The New Dress

And Other Stories

Virginia Woolf

T0346939

ALMA CLASSICS

ALMA CLASSICS
an imprint of

ALMA BOOKS LTD
Thornton House
Thornton Road
Wimbledon Village
London SW19 4NG
United Kingdom
www.almaclassics.com

For the publication date of each story, see the relevant endnote
This edition first published by Alma Classics in 2024

Cover: David Wardle

Printed in Great Britain by CPI Group (UK) Ltd, Croydon CR0 4YY

MIX
Paper | Supporting
responsible forestry
FSC® C171272

ISBN: 978-1-84749-910-3

Contents

Other books by VIRGINIA WOOLF
published by Alma Classics

*The New Dress
and Other Stories*

Solid Objects*

The only thing that moved upon the vast semicircle of the beach was one small black spot. As it came nearer to the ribs and spine of the stranded pilchard boat, it became apparent from a certain tenuity in its blackness that this spot possessed four legs, and moment by moment it became more unmistakable that it was composed of the persons of two young men. Even thus in outline against the sand there was an unmistakable vitality in them – an indescribable vigour in the approach and withdrawal of the bodies, slight though it was – which proclaimed some violent argument issuing from the tiny mouths of the little round heads. This was corroborated on closer view by the repeated lunging of a walking stick on the right-hand side. "You mean to tell me… You actually believe…" Thus the walking stick on the right-hand side next the waves seemed to be asserting as it cut long straight stripes on the sand.

"Politics be damned!" issued clearly from the body on the left-hand side, and, as these words were uttered, the mouths, noses, chins, little moustaches, tweed caps, rough boots, shooting coats and check stockings of the two speakers became clearer and clearer; the smoke of their pipes went up into the air; nothing was so solid, so living, so hard, red, hirsute and virile as these two bodies for miles and miles of sea and sandhill.

They flung themselves down by the six ribs and spine of the black pilchard boat. You know how the body seems to shake itself free from an argument and to apologize for a mood of exaltation, flinging itself down and expressing in the looseness of its attitude a readiness to take up with something new – whatever it may be that comes next to hand. So Charles, whose stick had been slashing the beach for half a mile or so, began skimming

3

flat pieces of slate over the water, and John, who had exclaimed "Politics be damned!", began burrowing his fingers down, down, into the sand. As his hand went further and further beyond the wrist, so that he had to hitch his sleeve a little higher, his eyes lost their intensity, or rather the background of thought and experience which gives an inscrutable depth to the eyes of grown people disappeared, leaving only the clear transparent surface, expressing nothing but wonder, which the eyes of young children display. No doubt the act of burrowing in the sand had something to do with it. He remembered that, after digging for a little, the water oozes round your fingertips; the hole then becomes a moat, a well, a spring, a secret channel to the sea. As he was choosing which of these things to make it, still working his fingers in the water, they curled round something hard – a full drop of solid matter – and gradually dislodged a large irregular lump, and brought it to the surface. When the sand coating was wiped off, a green tint appeared. It was a lump of glass, so thick as to be almost opaque; the smoothing of the sea had completely worn off any edge or shape, so that it was impossible to say whether it had been bottle, tumbler or window pane; it was nothing but glass; it was almost a precious stone. You had only to enclose it in a rim of gold or pierce it with a wire, and it became a jewel – part of a necklace, or a dull, green light upon a finger. Perhaps after all it was really a gem, something worn by a dark princess trailing her finger in the water as she sat in the stern of the boat and listened to the slaves singing as they rowed her across the bay. Or the oak sides of a sunk Elizabethan treasure chest had split apart, and, rolled over and over, over and over, its emeralds had come at last to shore. John turned it in his hands; he held it to the light; he held it so that its irregular mass blotted out the body and extended right arm of his friend. The green thinned and thickened slightly as it was held against the sky or against the body. It pleased him; it puzzled him; it was so hard, so concentrated, so definite an object compared with the vague sea and the hazy shore.

Now a sigh disturbed him – profound, final, making him aware that his friend Charles had thrown all the flat stones within reach, or had come to the conclusion that it was not worthwhile to throw them. They ate their sandwiches side by side. When they had done and were shaking themselves and rising to their feet, John took the lump of glass and looked at it in silence. Charles looked at it too. But he saw immediately that it was not flat, and filling his pipe he said with the energy that dismisses a foolish strain of thought:

"To return to what I was saying…"

He did not see, or if he had seen would hardly have noticed, that John, after looking at the lump for a moment as if in hesitation, slipped it inside his pocket. That impulse, too, may have been the impulse which leads a child to pick up one pebble on a path strewn with them, promising it a life of warmth and security upon the nursery mantelpiece, delighting in the sense of power and benignity which such an action confers, and believing that the heart of the stone leaps with joy when it sees itself chosen from a million like it, to enjoy this bliss instead of a life of cold and wet upon the high road. "It might so easily have been any other of the millions of stones, but it was I, I, I!"

Whether this thought or not was in John's mind, the lump of glass had its place upon the mantelpiece, where it stood heavy upon a little pile of bills and letters, and served not only as an excellent paperweight, but also as a natural stopping place for the young man's eyes when they wandered from his book. Looked at again and again half consciously by a mind thinking of something else, any object mixes itself so profoundly with the stuff of thought that it loses its actual form and recomposes itself a little differently in an ideal shape which haunts the brain when we least expect it. So John found himself attracted to the windows of curiosity shops when he was out walking, merely because he saw something which reminded him of the lump of glass. Anything, so long as it was an object of some kind, more or less round, perhaps with a dying flame deep-sunk in its mass, anything – china, glass, amber, rock, marble – even the smooth oval egg of a prehistoric bird would do.

He took, also, to keeping his eyes upon the ground, especially in the neighbourhood of wasteland where the household refuse is thrown away. Such objects often occurred there – thrown away, of no use to anybody, shapeless, discarded. In a few months he had collected four or five specimens that took their place upon the mantelpiece. They were useful, too, for a man who is standing for Parliament upon the brink of a brilliant career has any number of papers to keep in order – addresses to constituents, declarations of policy, appeals for subscriptions, invitations to dinner, and so on.

One day, starting from his rooms in the Temple* to catch a train in order to address his constituents, his eyes rested upon a remarkable object lying half hidden in one of those little borders of grass which edge the bases of vast legal buildings. He could only touch it with the point of his stick through the railings, but he could see that it was a piece of china of the most remarkable shape, as nearly resembling a starfish as anything – shaped, or broken accidentally, into five irregular but unmistakable points. The colouring was mainly blue, but green stripes or spots of some kind overlaid the blue, and lines of crimson gave it a richness and lustre of the most attractive kind. John was determined to possess it – but the more he pushed, the further it receded. At length he was forced to go back to his rooms and improvise a wire ring attached to the end of a stick, with which, by dint of great care and skill, he finally drew the piece of china within reach of his hands. As he seized hold of it, he exclaimed in triumph. At that moment the clock struck. It was out of the question that he should keep his appointment. The meeting was held without him. But how had the piece of china been broken into this remarkable shape? A careful examination put it beyond doubt that the star shape was accidental, which made it all the more strange, and it seemed unlikely that there should be another such in existence. Set at the opposite end of the mantelpiece from the lump of glass that had been dug from the sand, it looked like a creature from another world – freakish and fantastic as a harlequin. It seemed to be pirouetting through space, winking light like a fitful star.

The contrast between the china, so vivid and alert, and the glass, so mute and contemplative, fascinated him, and wondering and amazed he asked himself how the two came to exist in the same world, let alone to stand upon the same narrow strip of marble in the same room. The question remained unanswered.

He now began to haunt the places which are most prolific of broken china, such as pieces of wasteland between railway lines, sites of demolished houses and commons in the neighbourhood of London. But china is seldom thrown from a great height; it is one of the rarest of human actions. You have to find in conjunction a very high house and a woman of such reckless impulse and passionate prejudice that she flings her jar or pot straight from the window without thought of who is below. Broken china was to be found in plenty, but broken in some trifling domestic accident, without purpose or character. Nevertheless, he was often astonished, as he came to go into the question more deeply, by the immense variety of shapes to be found in London alone, and there was still more cause for wonder and speculation in the differences of qualities and designs. The finest specimens he would bring home and place upon his mantelpiece, where, however, their duty was more and more of an ornamental nature, since papers needing a weight to keep them down became scarcer and scarcer.

He neglected his duties, perhaps, or discharged them absent-mindedly, or his constituents when they visited him were unfavourably impressed by the appearance of his mantelpiece. At any rate, he was not elected to represent them in Parliament, and his friend Charles, taking it much to heart and hurrying to condole with him, found him so little cast down by the disaster that he could only suppose that it was too serious a matter for him to realize all at once.

In truth, John had been that day to Barnes Common, and there, under a furze bush, had found a very remarkable piece of iron. It was almost identical with the glass in shape, massy and globular, but so cold and heavy, so black and metallic, that it was evidently alien to the earth and had its origin in one of the dead stars or was itself the cinder of a moon. It weighed his pocket down; it weighed the mantelpiece down; it radiated cold. And yet the meteorite stood upon the same ledge with the lump of glass and the star-shaped china.

As his eyes passed from one to another, the determination to possess objects that even surpassed these tormented the young man. He devoted himself more and more resolutely to the search. If he had not been consumed by ambition and convinced that one day some newly discovered rubbish heap would reward him, the disappointments he had suffered, let alone the fatigue and derision, would have made him give up the pursuit. Provided with a bag and a long stick fitted with an adaptable hook, he ransacked all deposits of earth; raked beneath matted tangles of scrub; searched all alleys and spaces between walls where he had learnt to expect to find objects of this kind thrown away. As his standard became higher and his taste more severe, the disappointments were innumerable, but always some gleam of hope, some piece of china or glass curiously marked or broken, lured him on. Day after day passed. He was no longer young. His career – that is, his political career – was a thing of the past. People gave up visiting him. He was too silent to be worth asking to dinner. He never talked to anyone about his serious ambitions; their lack of understanding was apparent in their behaviour.

He leant back in his chair now and watched Charles lift the stones on the mantelpiece a dozen times and put them down emphatically to mark what he was saying about the conduct of the government, without once noticing their existence.

"What was the truth of it, John?" asked Charles suddenly, turning and facing him. "What made you give it up like that all in a second?"

"I've not given it up," John replied.

"But you've not a ghost of a chance now," said Charles roughly.

"I don't agree with you there," said John with conviction. Charles looked at him and was profoundly uneasy; the most extraordinary doubts possessed him; he had a queer sense that they were talking about different things. He looked round to find some relief for his horrible depression, but the disorderly appearance of the room depressed him still further. What was that stick, and the old carpet bag hanging against the wall? And then those stones? Looking at John, something fixed and distant in his expression alarmed him. He knew only too well that his mere appearance upon the platform was out of the question.

"Pretty stones," he said as cheerfully as he could, and saying that he had an appointment to keep, he left John – for ever.

In the Orchard*

Miranda slept in the orchard, lying in a long chair beneath the apple tree. Her book had fallen into the grass, and her finger still seemed to point at the sentence *"Ce pays est vraiment un des coins du monde où le rire des filles éclate le mieux..."** as if she had fallen asleep just there. The opals on her finger flushed green, flushed rosy and again flushed orange as the sun, oozing through the apple trees, filled them. Then, when the breeze blew, her purple dress rippled like a flower attached to a stalk; the grasses nodded, and the white butterfly came blowing this way and that just above her face.

Four feet in the air over her head the apples hung. Suddenly there was a shrill clamour as if they were gongs of cracked brass beaten violently, irregularly and brutally. It was only the schoolchildren saying the multiplication table in unison, stopped by the teacher, scolded and beginning to say the multiplication table over again. But this clamour passed four feet above Miranda's head, went through the apple boughs and, striking against the cowman's little boy, who was picking blackberries in the hedge when he should have been at school, made him tear his thumb on the thorns.

Next there was a solitary cry – sad, human, brutal. Old Parsley was, indeed, blind drunk.

Then the very topmost leaves of the apple tree, flat like little fish against the blue, thirty feet above the earth, chimed with a pensive and lugubrious note. It was the organ in the church playing one of *Hymns Ancient and Modern*.* The sound floated out and was cut into atoms by a flock of fieldfares flying at an enormous speed – somewhere or other. Miranda lay asleep thirty feet beneath.

Then above the apple tree and the pear tree two hundred feet above Miranda lying asleep in the orchard bells thudded, intermittent, sullen, didactic, for six poor women of the parish were being churched, and the rector was returning, thanks to Heaven.

And above that, with a sharp squeak, the golden feather of the church tower turned from south to east. The wind changed. Above everything else it droned – above the woods, the meadows, the hills – miles above Miranda lying in the orchard asleep. It swept on, eyeless, brainless, meeting nothing that could stand against it, until, wheeling the other way, it turned south again. Miles below, in a space as big as the eye of a needle, Miranda stood upright and cried aloud: "Oh, I shall be late for tea!"

Miranda slept in the orchard – or perhaps she was not asleep, for her lips moved very slightly, as if they were saying "*Ce pays est vraiment un des coins du monde... où le rire des filles... éclate... éclate... éclate...*" – and then she smiled and let her body sink all its weight onto the enormous earth which rises, she thought, to carry me on its back as if I were a leaf, or a queen (here the children said the multiplication table), or, Miranda went on, I might be lying on the top of a cliff with the gulls screaming above me. The higher they fly, she continued, as the teacher scolded the children and rapped Jimmy over the knuckles till they bled, the deeper they look into the sea... into the sea, she repeated, and her fingers relaxed and her lips closed gently as if she were floating on the sea, and then, when the shout of the drunken man sounded overhead, she drew breath with an extraordinary ecstasy, for she thought that she heard life itself crying out from a rough tongue in a scarlet mouth, from the wind, from the bells, from the curved green leaves of the cabbages.

Naturally she was being married when the organ played the tune from *Hymns Ancient and Modern*, and, when the bells rang after the six poor women had been churched, the sullen intermittent thud made her think that the very earth shook with the hoofs of the horse that was galloping towards her ("Ah, I have only to wait!" she sighed), and it seemed to her that everything had already begun moving, crying, riding, flying round her, across her, towards her in a pattern.

Mary is chopping the wood, she thought; Pearman is herding the cows; the carts are coming up from the meadows; the rider... and she traced out the lines that the men, the carts, the birds and the rider made over the countryside, until they all seemed driven out, round and across by the beat of her own heart.

Miles up in the air the wind changed; the golden feather of the church tower squeaked; and Miranda jumped up and cried: "Oh, I shall be late for tea!"

Miranda slept in the orchard – or was she asleep, or was she not asleep? Her purple dress stretched between the two apple trees. There were twenty-four apple trees in the orchard, some slanting slightly, others growing straight with a rush up the trunk which spread wide into branches and formed into round red or yellow drops. Each apple tree had sufficient space. The sky exactly fitted the leaves. When the breeze blew, the line of the boughs against the wall slanted slightly and then returned. A wagtail flew diagonally from one corner to another. Cautiously hopping, a thrush advanced towards a fallen apple; from the other wall a sparrow fluttered just above the grass. The uprush of the trees was tied down by these movements; the whole was compacted by the orchard walls. For miles beneath the earth was clamped together, rippled on the surface with wavering air, and across the corner of the orchard the blue-green was slit by a purple streak. The wind changing, one bunch of apples was tossed so high that it blotted out two cows in the meadow ("Oh, I shall be late for tea!" cried Miranda), and the apples hung straight across the wall again.

Mrs Dalloway in Bond Street*

Mrs Dalloway said she would buy the gloves herself.

Big Ben was striking as she stepped out into the street. It was eleven o'clock, and the unused hour was fresh, as if issued to children on a beach. But there was something solemn in the deliberate swing of the repeated strokes – something stirring in the murmur of wheels and the shuffle of footsteps.

No doubt they were not all bound on errands of happiness. There is much more to be said about us than that we walk the streets of Westminster. Big Ben too is nothing but steel rods consumed by rust, were it not for the care of HM's Office of Works. Only, for Mrs Dalloway the moment was complete – for Mrs Dalloway June was fresh. A happy childhood – and it was not to his daughters only that Justin Parry* had seemed a fine fellow (weak of course on the Bench); flowers at evening, smoke rising; the caw of rooks falling from ever so high, down, down through the October air – there is nothing to take the place of childhood. A leaf of mint brings it back – or a cup with a blue ring.

Poor little wretches, she sighed, and pressed forward. Oh, right under the horses' noses, you little demon! And there she was left on the kerb stretching her hand out, while Jimmy Dawes grinned on the farther side.

A charming woman – poised, eager, strangely white-haired for her pink cheeks – so Scope Purvis, CB,* saw her as he hurried to his office. She stiffened a little, waiting for Durtnall's van to pass. Big Ben struck the tenth, struck the eleventh stroke. The leaden circles dissolved in the air. Pride held her erect, inheriting, handing on, acquainted with discipline and with suffering. How people suffered, how they suffered, she thought, thinking of Mrs Foxcroft at the embassy last night, decked with jewels, eating her heart out because that nice boy was dead, and now the old Manor House (Durtnall's van passed) must go to a cousin.

"Good morning to you!" said Hugh Whitbread raising his hat rather extravagantly by the china shop, for they had known each other as children. "Where are you off to?"

"I love walking in London," said Mrs Dalloway. "Really it's better than walking in the country!"

"We've just come up," said Hugh Whitbread. "Unfortunately to see doctors."

"Milly?" said Mrs Dalloway, instantly compassionate.

"Out of sorts," said Hugh Whitbread. "That sort of thing. Dick all right?"

"First-rate!" said Clarissa.

Of course, she thought, walking on, Milly is about my age – fifty, fifty-two. So it is probably *that*. Hugh's manner had said so, said it perfectly... dear old Hugh, thought Mrs Dalloway, remembering with amusement, with gratitude, with emotion, how shy, like a brother – one would rather die than speak to one's brother – Hugh had always been, when he was at Oxford and came over, and perhaps one of them (drat the thing!) couldn't ride. How then could women sit in Parliament? How could they do things with men? For there is this extraordinarily deep instinct, something inside one – you can't get over it, it's no use trying – and men like Hugh respect it without our saying it, which is what one loves, thought Clarissa, in dear old Hugh.

She had passed through the Admiralty Arch and saw at the end of the empty road with its thin trees Victoria's white mound,* Victoria's billowing motherliness, amplitude and homeliness, always ridiculous, yet how sublime, thought Mrs Dalloway, remembering Kensington Gardens and the old lady in horn spectacles and being told by Nanny to stop dead still and bow to the queen. The flag flew above the palace. The king and queen* were back, then. Dick had met her at lunch the other day – a thoroughly nice woman. It matters so much to the poor, thought Clarissa, and to the soldiers. A man in bronze stood heroically on a pedestal with a gun on her left-hand side – the South African War.* It matters, thought Mrs Dalloway walking towards Buckingham Palace. There it stood four-square, in the broad sunshine, uncompromising, plain. But it was character, she thought, something inborn in the race, what Indians respected. The queen went to hospitals, opened bazaars – the queen of England, thought Clarissa, looking at the palace. Already at this hour a motor car passed out at the gates; soldiers saluted; the gates were shut. And Clarissa, crossing the road, entered the park,* holding herself upright.

June had drawn out every leaf on the trees. The mothers of Westminster with mottled breasts gave suck to their young. Quite respectable girls lay stretched on the grass. An elderly man, stooping very stiffly, picked up a crumpled paper, spread it out flat and flung it away. How horrible! Last night at the embassy Sir Dighton* had said, "If I want a fellow to hold my horse, I have only to put up my hand." But the religious question is far more serious than the economic, Sir Dighton had said, which she thought extraordinarily interesting, from a man like Sir Dighton. "Oh, the country will never know what it has lost," he had said, talking of his own accord, about dear Jack Stewart.

She mounted the little hill lightly. The air stirred with energy. Messages were passing from the Fleet to the Admiralty. Piccadilly and Arlington Street and The Mall seemed to chafe the very air in the park and lift its leaves hotly, brilliantly, upon waves of that divine vitality which Clarissa loved. To ride, to dance – she had adored all that. Or going long walks in the country, talking, about books, what to do with one's life, for young people were amazingly priggish – oh, the things one had said! But one had conviction. Middle age is the devil. People like Jack'll never know that, she thought, for he never once thought of death – never, they said, knew he was dying. And now can never mourn – how did it go? – a head grown grey... From the contagion of the world's slow stain...* Have drunk their cup a round or two before...* From the contagion of the world's slow stain! She held herself upright.

But how Jack would have shouted! Quoting Shelley, in Piccadilly! "You want a pin," he would have said. He hated frumps. "My God, Clarissa! My God, Clarissa!" – she could hear him now at the Devonshire House party, about poor Sylvia Hunt in her amber necklace and that dowdy old silk. Clarissa held herself upright, for she had spoken aloud, and now she was in Piccadilly, passing the house with the slender green columns and the balconies; passing club windows full of newspapers; passing old Lady Burdett-Coutts's house, where the glazed white parrot used to hang; and Devonshire House, without its gilt leopards; and Claridge's, where she must remember Dick wanted her to leave a card on Mrs Jepson, or she would be gone. Rich Americans can be very charming. There was St James's Palace, like a child's game with bricks, and now – she had passed Bond Street – she was by Hatchard's bookshop. The stream was endless... endless... endless. Lords, Ascot, Hurlingham – what was it? What a duck, she thought, looking at the frontispiece of some book of memoirs spread wide in the bow window, Sir Joshua perhaps, or Romney...* arch, bright, demure... the sort of girl – like her own Elizabeth – the only *real* sort of girl. And there was that absurd book, *Soapy Sponge*,* which Jim used to quote by the yard, and Shakespeare's *Sonnets*. She knew them by heart. Phil and she had argued all day about the Dark Lady, and Dick had said straight out at dinner that night that he had never heard of her. Really, she had married him for that! He had never read Shakespeare! There must be some little cheap book she could buy for Milly – *Cranford** of course! Was there ever anything so enchanting as the cow in petticoats?* If only people had that sort of humour, that sort of self-respect now, thought Clarissa, for she remembered the broad pages, the sentences' ending, the characters – how one talked about them as if they were real. For all the great things one must go to the past, she thought. From the contagion of the world's slow stain... Fear no more the heat o' the sun...* And now can never mourn, can never mourn, she repeated, her eyes straying over the window, for it ran in her head; the test of great poetry; the moderns had never written anything one wanted to read about death, she thought, and turned.

Omnibuses joined motor cars; motor cars vans; vans taxicabs, taxicabs motor cars – here was an open motor car with a girl, alone. Up till four, her feet tingling, I know, thought Clarissa, for the girl looked washed out, half asleep, in the corner of the car after the dance. And another car came – and another. No! No! No! Clarissa smiled good-naturedly. The fat lady had taken every sort of trouble, but diamonds! Orchids! At this hour of the morning! No! No! No! The excellent policeman would, when the time came, hold up his hand. Another motor car passed. How utterly unattractive! Why should a girl of that age paint black round her eyes? And a young man with a girl, at this hour, when the country... The admirable policeman raised his hand, and Clarissa, acknowledging his sway, taking her time, crossed, walked towards Bond Street, saw the narrow crooked street, the yellow banners, the thick notched telegraph wires stretched across the sky.

A hundred years ago her great-great-grandfather, Seymour Parry, who ran away with Conway's daughter, had walked down Bond Street. Down Bond Street the Parrys had walked for a hundred years, and might have met the Dalloways (Leighs on the mother's side) going up. Her father got his clothes from Hill's. There was a roll of cloth in the window, and here just one jar on a black table, incredibly expensive – like the thick pink salmon on the ice block at the fishmonger's. The jewels were exquisite – pink and orange stars, paste, Spanish, she thought, and chains of old gold, starry buckles, little brooches which had been worn on sea-green satin by ladies with high headdresses. But no good looking! One must economize. She must go on past the picture dealer's where one of the odd French pictures hung, as if people had thrown confetti – pink and blue – for a joke. If you had lived with pictures (and it's the same with books and music), thought Clarissa, passing the Aeolian Hall,* you can't be taken in by a joke.

The river of Bond Street was clogged. There, like a queen at a tournament, raised, regal, was Lady Bexborough. She sat in her carriage, upright, alone, looking through her glasses. The white glove was loose at her wrist. She was in black, quite shabby, yet, thought Clarissa, how extraordinarily it tells, breeding, self-respect, never saying a word too much or letting people gossip – an astonishing friend: no one can pick a hole in her after all these years – and now, there she is, thought Clarissa, passing the countess, who waited powdered, perfectly still, and Clarissa would have given anything to be like that, the mistress of Clarefield, talking politics like a man. But she never goes anywhere, thought Clarissa, and it's quite useless to ask her, and the carriage went on and Lady Bexborough was borne past like a queen at a tournament, though she had nothing to live for and the old man is failing and they say she is sick of it all, thought Clarissa, and the tears actually rose to her eyes as she entered the shop.

"Good morning," said Clarissa in her charming voice. "Gloves," she said with her exquisite friendliness, and putting her bag on the counter began, very slowly, to undo the buttons. "White gloves," she said. "Above the elbow." And she looked straight into the shop woman's face – but this was not the girl she remembered... She looked quite old. "These really don't fit," said Clarissa. The shop girl looked at them. "Madam wears bracelets?" Clarissa spread out her fingers. "Perhaps it's my rings." And the girl took the grey gloves with her to the end of the counter.

Yes, thought Clarissa, if it's the girl I remember, she's twenty years older... There was only one other customer, sitting sideways at the counter, her elbow poised, her bare hand drooping, vacant – like a figure on a Japanese fan, thought Clarissa, too vacant perhaps, yet some men would adore her. The lady shook her head sadly. Again the gloves were too large. She turned round the glass. "Above the wrist," she reproached the grey-headed woman, who looked and agreed.

They waited; a clock ticked; Bond Street hummed, dulled, distant; the woman went away holding gloves. "Above the wrist," said the lady mournfully, raising her voice. And she would have to order chairs, ices, flowers and cloakroom tickets, thought Clarissa.

The people she didn't want would come; the others wouldn't. She would stand by the door. They sold stockings – silk stockings. A lady is known by her gloves and her shoes, old Uncle William used to say. And through the hanging silk stockings quivering silver she looked at the lady, sloping-shouldered, her hand drooping, her bag slipping, her eyes vacantly on the floor. It would be intolerable if dowdy women came to her party! Would one have liked Keats if he had worn red socks? Oh, at last... She drew into the counter, and it flashed into her mind:

"Do you remember before the war you had gloves with pearl buttons?"

"French gloves, madam?"

"Yes, they were French," said Clarissa. The other lady rose very sadly and took her bag, and looked at the gloves on the counter. But they were all too large – always too large at the wrist.

"With pearl buttons," said the shop girl, who looked ever so much older. She split the lengths of tissue paper apart on the counter. With pearl buttons, thought Clarissa, perfectly simple – how French!

"Madam's hands are so slender," said the shop girl, drawing the glove firmly, smoothly, down over her rings. And Clarissa looked at her arm in the looking glass. The glove hardly came to the elbow. Were there others half an inch longer? Still it seemed tiresome to bother her – perhaps the one day in the month, thought Clarissa, when it's an agony to stand. "Oh, don't bother," she said. But the gloves were brought.

"Don't you get fearfully tired," she said in her charming voice, "standing? When d'you get your holiday?"

"In September, madam, when we're not so busy."

When we're in the country, thought Clarissa. Or shooting. She has a fortnight at Brighton. In some stuffy lodging. The landlady takes the sugar. Nothing would be easier than to send her to Mrs Lumley's right in the country (and it was on the tip of her tongue). But then she remembered how on their honeymoon Dick had shown her the folly of giving impulsively. It was much more important, he said, to get trade with China. Of course he was right. And she could feel the girl wouldn't like to be given things. There she was in her place. So was Dick. Selling gloves was her job. She had her own sorrows quite separate... "And now can never mourn, can never mourn", the words ran in her head. "From the contagion of the world's slow stain," thought Clarissa, holding her arm stiff, for there are moments when it seems utterly futile (the glove was drawn off, leaving her arm flecked with powder) – simply one doesn't believe, thought Clarissa, any more in God.

The traffic suddenly roared; the silk stockings brightened. A customer came in.

"White gloves," she said, with some ring in her voice that Clarissa remembered.

It used, thought Clarissa, to be so simple. Down, down through the air came the caw of the rooks. When Sylvia died, hundreds of years ago, the yew hedges looked so lovely with the diamond webs in the mist before early church. But if Dick were to die tomorrow... As for believing in God – no, she would let the children choose, but for herself, like Lady Bexborough, who opened the bazaar, they say, with the telegram in her hand (Roden, her favourite, killed), she would go on. But why, if one doesn't believe? For the sake of others, she thought, taking the glove in her hand. The girl would be much more unhappy if she didn't believe.

"Thirty shillings," said the shop woman. "No, pardon me, madam, thirty-five. The French gloves are more."

For one doesn't live for oneself, thought Clarissa.

And then the other customer took a glove, tugged it, and it split.

"There!" she exclaimed.

"A fault of the skin," said the grey-headed woman hurriedly. "Sometimes a drop of acid in tanning. Try this pair, madam."

"But it's an awful swindle to ask two pound ten!"

Clarissa looked at the lady; the lady looked at Clarissa.

"Gloves have never been quite so reliable since the war," said the shop girl, apologizing, to Clarissa.

But where had she seen the other lady?... Elderly, with a frill under her chin; wearing a black ribbon for gold eyeglasses; sensual, clever, like a Sargent* drawing. How one can tell from a voice when people are in the habit, thought Clarissa, of making other people – "It's a shade too tight," she said – obey. The shop woman went off again. Clarissa was left waiting. Fear no more, she repeated, playing her finger on the counter. Fear no more the heat o' the sun. Fear no more, she repeated. There were little brown spots on her arm. And the girl crawled like a snail. Thou thy worldly task hast done.* Thousands of young men had died that things might go on. At last! Half an inch above the elbow; pearl buttons; five and a quarter. My dear slowcoach, thought Clarissa, do you think I can sit here the whole morning? Now you'll take twenty-five minutes to bring me my change!

There was a violent explosion in the street outside.* The shop women cowered behind the counters. But Clarissa, sitting very upright, smiled at the other lady. "Miss Anstruther!" she exclaimed.

Ancestors*

Mrs Vallance, as she replied to Jack Renshaw, who had made that rather silly remark of his about not liking to watch cricket matches, wished that she could make him understand somehow what became every moment more obvious at a party like this: that if her father had been alive, people would have realized how foolish, how wicked – no, not so much wicked as silly and ugly – how, compared to really dignified simple men and women like her father, like her dear mother, all this seemed to her so trivial. How very different his mind was, and his life – and her mother – and how differently, entirely differently she herself had been brought up.

"Here we all are," she said suddenly, "cooped up here in one room the size of an oven, when up in Scotland where I was born we should all be..." She owed it to these foolish young men, who were after all quite nice, though a little undersized, to make them understand what her father, what her mother and she herself too, for she was like them at heart, felt. And then it came over her in a rush, how she owed it to the world to make men understand how her father and her mother – how she too – were quite different.

He had stopped in Edinburgh for a night once, Mr Renshaw said.

"Was she Scotch?" he asked.

He did not know then who her father was, that she was John Ellis Rattray's daughter and her mother was Catherine Macdonald – and one night in Edinburgh! And she had spent all those wonderful years there, there and at Elliotshaw on the Northumbrian border. There she had run wild among the currant bushes; there her father's friends had come and, only a girl as she was, she had heard the most wonderful talk of her time. She could see them still: her father, Sir Duncan Clements, Mr Rogers (old Mr Rogers was her ideal of a Greek sage) sitting under the cedar tree, after dinner in the starlight.

They talked about everything in the world, it seemed to her now; they were too large-minded ever to laugh at other people; they had taught her, though she was only a girl, how to revere beauty. What was there beautiful in this stuffy London room?

"Oh, those poor flowers!" she exclaimed. For a carnation or two were actually trodden underfoot, for petals of flowers were all crumpled and crushed. For she felt almost too much for flowers. Her mother had loved flowers: ever since she was a child, she had been brought up to feel that to hurt a flower was to hurt the most exquisite thing in nature. Nature had always been a passion with her – the mountains, the sea. And here in London one looked out of the window and saw more houses. One had a dreadful sense of human beings packed on top of each other in little boxes. It was an atmosphere in which she could not possibly live – herself – now she could not bear to walk in London and see the children in the streets. She was perhaps too sensitive; life would be impossible if everyone was like her, but when she remembered her own childhood, and her father and mother, and the beauty and care that were lavished on them...

"What a lovely frock!" said Jack Renshaw – and that seemed to her altogether wrong, for a young man to be noticing women's clothes at all. Her father was full of reverence for women, but he never thought of noticing what they wore. And of all these girls (the girls might be pretty), there was not a single one of them one could call beautiful – as she remembered her mother, her dear stately mother, who never seemed to dress differently summer or winter, whether they had people or not, but always looked herself in some lace and a black dress, or, as she grew older, a little cap. When she was a widow, she would sit among her flowers by the hour, and she seemed to be more with ghosts than with them all, dreaming of the past – which is, Mrs Vallance thought, somehow so much more real than the present. But why?

It is in the past, with those wonderful men and women, she thought, that I really live – it is they who knew me, it is those people only (and she thought of the starlit garden and the trees and old Mr Rogers, and her father, in his white linen coat, smoking) who understood me. She felt her eyes soften and deepen as at the approach of tears, standing there in Mrs Dalloway's drawing room, looking at these people, these flowers, this noisy, bright, chattering crowd – at herself, that little girl who was to travel so far, running, picking sweet Alice,* then sitting up in bed in the attic, which smelt of pinewood, reading stories, poetry. She had read all Shelley between the age of twelve and fifteen, and used to say it to her father, holding her hands behind her back, while he shaved.* The tears began, down in the back of her head, to rise as she looked at this picture of herself, and added the suffering of a lifetime (she had suffered abominably: life had passed over her like a wheel, life was not what it had seemed then – it was like this party) to the child standing there, reciting Shelley, with her dark wild eyes. But what had they not seen later!

And it was only those people, dead now, laid away in quiet Scotland, who had ever seen all that she had it in her to be, who had known her, who knew what she had it in her to be. And now the tears came closer as she thought of the little girl in the cotton frock... how large and dark her eyes were; how beautiful she looked repeating the 'Ode to the West Wind';* how proud her father was of her, and how great he was, and how great her mother even; and how, when she was with them, she was entirely so pure, so good, so gifted that she had it in her to be anything – that if they had lived and she had always been with them in the garden (which now appeared the only place where she had spent her whole childhood, and it was always starlit, and always summer, and they were always sitting out under the cedar tree smoking, except that somehow her mother was dreaming alone, in her widow's cap, among her flowers – and how good and kind and respectful the old servants were... Andrews the gardener, Jersy the cook... and old Sultan, the Newfoundland dog... and the vine, and the pond, and the pump... and...) – Mrs Vallance, looking very fierce and proud and satirical, compared her life with other people's lives – and if that life could have gone on for ever, then Mrs Vallance felt none of this (and she looked at Jack Renshaw and the girl whose clothes he admired), could have had any existence, and she would have been oh perfectly happy, perfectly good... instead of which, here she was forced to listen to a young man saying... And she laughed almost scornfully – and yet tears were in her eyes – that he could not bear to watch cricket matches!

The Introduction*

Lily Everit saw Mrs Dalloway bearing down on her from the other side of the room, and could have prayed her not to come and disturb her – and yet, as Mrs Dalloway approached with her right hand raised and a smile which Lily knew (though this was her first party) meant "But you've got to come out of your corner and talk", a smile at once benevolent and drastic, she felt the strangest mixture of excitement and fear, of desire to be left alone and of longing to be taken out and thrown into the boiling depths. But Mrs Dalloway was intercepted, caught by an old gentleman with white moustaches. So Lily Everit had two minutes' respite there in which to hug to herself, as a drowning man might hug a spar in the sea, her essay on the character of Dean Swift.* It had been given back to her that morning by Professor Miller, marked with three red stars: first-rate. First-rate – she repeated that to herself; she took a sip of that cordial that was ever so much weaker now than it had been when she stood before the long glass being finished off (a pat here, a dab there) by her sister and Mildred, the housemaid. For as their hands moved about her, she felt that they were fidgeting agreeably on the surface, but beneath lay untouched, like a lump of glowing metal, her essay on the character of Dean Swift – and all their praises when she came downstairs and stood in the hall waiting for a cab (Rupert had come out of his room and said what a swell she looked) ruffled the surface, went like a breeze among ribbons, but no more. Essays were the facts of life.

One divided life (she felt sure of it) into fact and into fiction, into rock and into wave, she thought, driving along and seeing things with such intensity that for ever and ever she would see the driver's back through the glass and her own white phantom reflected in his dark coat. Then, as she came into the house, at the very first

sight of people moving upstairs and downstairs, this hard lump
(her essay on the character of Swift) wobbled, began melting* –
she could not keep hold of it, and all her being (no longer sharp
as a diamond cleaving the heart of life asunder) turned to a mist
of alarm, apprehension and defence as she stood at bay in her
corner. This was the famous place: the world.

Looking out, Lily Everit instinctively hid that essay of hers,
so ashamed was she now, so bewildered too, and on tiptoe
nevertheless, to adjust her focus and get into right proportions (the
old had been shamefully wrong) these diminishing and increasing
things (what could one call them?... people – impressions of
people's lives?) which seemed to menace and mount over her,
to turn everything to water, leaving her only the power to stand
at bay.

Now Mrs Dalloway, who had never quite dropped her arm, had
shown by the way she moved it that she was coming, left the old
soldier with white moustaches and came straight down on her,
and said to the shy, charming girl with the clear eyes, the dark hair
which clustered poetically round her head and the thin body in a
dress which seemed to be slipping off, "Come and let me introduce
you" – and there Mrs Dalloway hesitated, and then, remembering
that Lily was the clever one who read poetry, looked about for
some young man, some young man just down from Oxford, who
would have read everything and would talk about himself. And
holding Lily Everit's hand, she led her towards a group where
there were young people talking.

Lily Everit hung back a little, might have been in the wake of a
steamer – felt, as Mrs Dalloway led her on, that it was now going
to happen, that nothing could prevent it, or save her (and she only
wanted it to be over now) from being flung into a whirlpool where
either she would perish or be saved. But what was the whirlpool?

Oh, it was made of a million things, and each so distinct to
her: Westminster Abbey; the sense of enormously high solemn
buildings surrounding them; grown up; being a woman. Perhaps
that was the thing that came out, that remained; it was partly

the dress, but all the little chivalries* and respects of the drawing room – all made her feel that she had come out of her chrysalis and was being proclaimed what in the long, comfortable darkness of childhood she had never been: this frail and beautiful creature, this limited and circumscribed creature who could not do what she liked, this butterfly with a thousand facets to its eyes and delicate fine plumage, and difficulties and sensibilities and sadnesses innumerable – a woman.

As she walked with Mrs Dalloway across the room, she accepted the part which was now laid on her, and, naturally, overdid it a little, as a soldier proud of the traditions of an old and famous uniform might overdo it, feeling conscious as she walked of her finery, of her tight shoes, of her coiled and twisted hair, and how if she dropped a handkerchief (this had happened with strangers) a man would stoop precipitately and give it to her – thus accentuating the delicacy, the artificiality of her bearing unnaturally, for they were not hers after all.

Hers it was, rather, to run and hurry and ponder on long solitary walks, climbing gates, stepping through the mud, and, through the blur, the dream, the ecstasy of loneliness, to see the plovers wheel and surprise the rabbits, and come in the hearts of woods or wide lonely moors upon little ceremonies which had no audience, private rites, pure beauty offered by beetles and lilies of the valley and dead leaves and still pools, without any care whatever what human beings thought of them, which filled her mind with rapture and wonder... all this was, until tonight, her ordinary being, by which she knew and liked herself and crept into the heart of mother and father and brothers and sisters – and this other was a flower which had opened in ten minutes. And with the flower opened there came too, incontrovertibly, its world, so different, so strange: the towers of Westminster; the high and formal buildings; the talk; this civilization, she felt, hanging back, as Mrs Dalloway led her on; this regulated way of life, which fell like a yoke about her neck, softly, indomitably, from the skies, a statement which there was no gainsaying.

Glancing at her essay, the three red stars dulled to obscurity, but peacefully, pensively, as if yielding to the pressure of unquestionable might – that is, the conviction that it was not hers to dominate or to assert, rather to air and embellish this orderly life where all was done already: high towers, solemn bells, flats built every brick of them by men's toil, parliaments too – and even the criss-cross of telegraph wires, she thought, looking at the window as she walked. What had she to oppose to this massive masculine achievement? An essay on the character of Dean Swift! And she came to the group, which Bob Brinsley dominated (with his heel on the fender and his head back), with his great honest forehead and his look of self-assurance – and his delicacy, and honour, and robust physical well-being, and sunburn, and airiness and direct descent from Shakespeare – what could she do but lay her essay, oh and the whole of her being, on the floor as a cloak for him to trample on, as a rose for him to rifle? Which she did, emphatically, when Mrs Dalloway said, still holding her hand as if she would run away from this supreme trial, this introduction, "Mr Brinsley – Miss Everit. Both of you love Shelley." But hers was not love compared with his.

Saying this, Mrs Dalloway felt, as she always felt remembering her youth, absurdly moved – youth meeting youth at her party, and there flashing, as at the concussion of steel upon flint (both stiffened to her feeling perceptibly), the loveliest and most ancient of all fires as she saw in Bob Brinsley's change of expression from carelessness to conformity to formality as he shook hands, which foreboded, Clarissa thought, the tenderness, the goodness, the carefulness* of women latent in all men, to her a sight to bring tears to the eyes, as it moved her even more intimately to see in Lily herself the shy look, the startled look, surely the loveliest of all looks on a girl's face, and man feeling this for woman, and woman that for man, and there flowing from that contact all those homes, trials, sorrows, profound joy and ultimate* staunchness in the face of catastrophe... Humanity was sweet at its heart, thought Clarissa, and her own life (to introduce a couple made her think of meeting Richard for the first time!) infinitely blessed. And on she went.

But, thought Lily Everit. But... but... but what?

Oh, nothing, she thought, hastily smothering down softly her sharp instinct. In the direct line from Shakespeare, she thought, and parliaments and churches, she thought, oh, and the telegraph wires too, she thought, and ostentatiously of set purpose begged Mr Brinsley to believe her implicitly when she offered him her essay upon the character of Dean Swift to do what he liked with, trample upon and destroy – for how could a mere child understand even for an instant the character of Dean Swift? Yes, she said. She did like reading.

"And I suppose you write?" he said. "Poems, presumably?"

"Essays," she said. And she would not let this horror get possession of her. She wanted to have her handkerchief picked up on the staircase and be a butterfly. Churches and parliaments, flats, even the telegraph wires – all, she told herself, made by men of toil, and this young man, she told herself, is in direct descent from Shakespeare, so she would not let this terror, this suspicion of something different, get hold of her and shrivel up her wings and drive her out into loneliness. But as she said this, she saw him (how else could she describe it?) kill a fly. That was it. He tore the wings off a fly, standing with his foot on the fender, his head thrown back, talking insolently about himself, arrogantly. But she didn't mind how insolent and arrogant he was to her, if only he had not been brutal to flies.

But she said, fidgeting as she smothered down that idea, why not, since he is the greatest of all worldly objects? And to worship, to adorn, to embellish was her task, her wings were for that. But he talked, but he looked, but he laughed – he tore the wings off a fly. He pulled the wings off its back with his clever strong hands, and she saw him do it – and she could not hide the knowledge from herself. But it is necessary that it should be so, she argued, thinking of the churches, of the parliaments and the blocks of flats, and so tried to crouch and cower and fold the wings down flat on her back.

But... but... what was it, why was it? In spite of all she could do, her essay upon the character of Swift became more and more obtrusive and the three stars burned quite bright again, only with a terrible lustre, no longer clear and brilliant, but troubled and bloodstained, as if this man, this great Mr Brinsley, had just, by pulling the wings off a fly as he talked (about his essay, about himself and once, laughing, about a girl there), charged her light being with cloud and confused her for ever and ever and shrivelled her wings on her back – and, as he turned away from her, she went nearer to the window and thought of the towers and civilization with horror, and the yoke that had fallen from the skies onto her neck crushed her, and she felt like a naked wretch who, having sought shelter in some shady garden, is turned out and made to understand (ah, but there was a kind of passion in it too) that there are no sanctuaries or butterflies, and this civilization, said Lily Everit to herself, as she accepted the kind compliments of old Mrs Bromley on her appearance, depends upon me. Mrs Bromley said later that, like all the Everits, Lily looked "as if she had the weight of the world upon her shoulders".

Together and Apart*

Mrs Dalloway introduced them, saying: you will like him. The conversation began some minutes before anything was said, for both Mr Serle and Miss Anning looked at the sky and in both of their minds the sky went on pouring its meaning, though very differently, until the presence of Mr Serle by her side became so distinct to Miss Anning that she could not see the sky simply, itself, any more, but the sky shored up by the tall body, dark eyes, grey hair, clasped hands, the stern melancholy (but she had been told "falsely melancholy") face of Roderick Serle – and, knowing how foolish it was, she yet felt impelled to say:

"What a beautiful night!"

Foolish! Idiotically foolish! But if one mayn't be foolish at the age of forty in the presence of the sky, which makes the wisest imbecile, mere wisps of straw, she and Mr Serle atoms, motes, standing there at Mrs Dalloway's window, and their lives, seen by moonlight, as long as an insect's and no more important.

"Well!" said Miss Anning, patting the sofa cushion emphatically. And down he sat beside her. Was he "falsely melancholy", as they said? Prompted by the sky, which seemed to make it all a little futile – what they said, what they did – she said something perfectly commonplace again:

"There was a Miss Serle who lived at Canterbury when I was a girl there."

With the sky in his mind, all the tombs of his ancestors immediately appeared to Mr Serle in a blue romantic light, and his eyes expanding and darkening, he said: "Yes."

"We are originally a Norman family, who came over with the Conqueror.* There is a Richard Serle buried in the cathedral. He was a Knight of the Garter."

Miss Anning felt that she had struck accidentally the true man upon whom the false man was built. Under the influence of the moon (the moon which symbolized man to her – she could see it through a chink of the curtain, and she took dips of the moon) she was capable of saying almost anything, and she settled in to disinter the true man who was buried under the false, saying to herself: "On, Stanley, on"* – which was a watchword of hers, a secret spur or scourge, such as middle-aged people often make to flagellate some inveterate vice, hers being a deplorable timidity, or rather indolence, for it was not so much that she lacked courage, but lacked energy, especially in talking to men, who frightened her rather, and so often her talks petered out into dull commonplaces, and she had very few men friends – very few intimate friends at all, she thought, but after all, did she want them? No. She had Sarah, Arthur, the cottage, the chow and, of course, *that*, she thought, dipping herself, sousing herself, even as she sat on the sofa beside Mr Serle, in *that*, in the sense she had coming home of something collected there, a cluster of miracles which she could not believe other people had (since it was she only who had Arthur, Sarah, the cottage and the chow), and* she soused herself again in the deep satisfactory possession, feeling that what with this and the moon (music that was, the moon), she could afford to leave this man and that pride of his in the Serles buried. No! That was the danger – she must not sink into torpidity – not at her age. "On, Stanley, on," she said to herself, and asked him:

"Do you know Canterbury yourself?"

Did he know Canterbury! Mr Serle smiled, thinking how absurd a question it was... how little she knew – this nice quiet woman who played some instrument and seemed intelligent and had good eyes, and was wearing a nice old necklace – knew what it meant. To be asked if he knew Canterbury – when the best years of his life, all his memories, things he had never been able to tell anybody, but had tried to write... ah, had tried to write (and he sighed) – all had centred in Canterbury; it made him laugh.

His sigh and then his laugh, his melancholy and his humour, made people like him, and he knew it, and yet being liked had not made up for the disappointment, and if he sponged on the liking people had for him (paying long calls on sympathetic ladies – long, long calls), it was half bitterly, for he had never done a tenth part of what he could have done and had dreamt of doing as a boy in Canterbury. With a stranger he felt a renewal of hope because they could not say that he had not done what he had promised, and yielding to his charm would give him a fresh start – at fifty! She had touched the spring. Fields and flowers and grey buildings dripped down into his mind, formed silver drops on the gaunt, dark walls of his mind and dripped down. With such an image his poems often began. He felt the desire to make images now, sitting by this quiet woman.

"Yes, I know Canterbury," he said reminiscently, sentimentally, inviting, Miss Anning felt, discreet questions, and that was what made him interesting to so many people, and it was this extraordinary facility and responsiveness to talk on his part that had been his undoing – so he thought, often, taking his studs out and putting his keys and small change on the dressing table after one of these parties (and he went out sometimes almost every night in the season), and, going down to breakfast, becoming quite different, grumpy, unpleasant at breakfast to his wife, who was an invalid and never went out, but had old friends to see her sometimes, women friends for the most part, interested in Indian philosophy and different cures and different doctors, which Roderick Serle snubbed off by some caustic remark too clever for her to meet, except by gentle expostulations and a tear or two... He had failed, he often thought, because he could not cut himself off utterly from society and the company of women, which was so necessary to him, and write. He had involved himself too deep in life – and here he would cross his knees (all his movements were a little unconventional and distinguished) and not blame himself, but put the blame off upon the richness of his nature, which he compared favourably with Wordsworth's,* for example, and, since he had given so much to people, he felt, resting his head on his hands, they in their turn should help him, and this was the prelude, tremulous, fascinating, exciting, to talk, and images bubbled up in his mind.

"She's like a fruit tree – like a flowering cherry tree," he said, looking at a youngish woman with fine white hair. It was a nice sort of image, Ruth Anning thought – rather nice, yet she did not feel sure that she liked this distinguished, melancholy man with his gestures – and it's odd, she thought, how one's feelings are influenced. She did not like *him*, though she rather liked that comparison of his of a woman to a cherry tree. Fibres of her were floated capriciously this way and that, like the tentacles of a sea anemone, now thrilled, now snubbed, and her brain, miles away, cool and distant, up in the air, received messages which it would sum up in time so that, when people talked about Roderick Serle (and he was a bit of a figure), she would say unhesitatingly "I like him" or "I don't like him", and her opinion would be made up for ever. An odd thought – a solemn thought – throwing a queer light on what human fellowship consisted of.

"It's odd that you should know Canterbury," said Mr Serle. "It's always a shock," he went on (the white-haired lady having passed), "when one meets someone" (they had never met before) "by chance, as it were, who touches the fringe of what has meant a great deal to oneself – touches accidentally, for I suppose Canterbury was nothing but a nice old town to you. So you stayed there one summer with an aunt?" (That was all Ruth Anning was going to tell him about her visit to Canterbury.) "And you saw the sights and went away and never thought of it again."

Let him think so – not liking him, she wanted him to run away with an absurd idea of her. For really, her three months in Canterbury had been amazing. She remembered to the last detail, though it was merely a chance visit, going to see Miss Charlotte Serle, an acquaintance of her aunt's. Even now she could repeat* Miss Serle's very words about the thunder. "Whenever I wake and hear thunder in the night, I think 'Someone has

35

been killed'." And she could see the hard, hairy, diamond-patterned carpet, and the twinkling, suffused, brown eyes of the elderly lady, holding the teacup out unfilled, while she said that about the thunder. And always she saw Canterbury, all thundercloud and livid apple blossom, and the long grey backs of the buildings.

The thunder roused her from her plethoric middle-aged swoon of indifference. "On, Stanley, on," she said to herself – that is, this man shall not glide away from me, like everybody else, on this false assumption: I will tell him the truth.

"I loved Canterbury," she said.

He kindled instantly. It was his gift, his fault, his destiny.

"Loved it," he repeated. "I can see that you did."

Her tentacles sent back the message that Roderick Serle was nice.

Their eyes met – collided rather, for each felt that behind the eyes the secluded being who sits in darkness while his shallow agile companion does all the tumbling and beckoning and keeps the show going suddenly stood erect, flung off his cloak, confronted the other. It was alarming – it was terrific. They were elderly and burnished into a glowing smoothness, so that Roderick Serle would go, perhaps to a dozen parties in a season, and feel nothing out of the common, or only sentimental regrets, and the desire for pretty images – like this of the flowering cherry tree – and all the time there stagnated in him unstirred a sort of superiority to his company, a sense of untapped resources, which sent him back home dissatisfied with his life, with himself, yawning, empty, capricious. But now, quite suddenly, like a white bolt in a mist (but this image forged itself with the inevitability of lightning and loomed up), there it had happened, the old ecstasy of life, its invincible assault – for it was unpleasant, at the same time that it rejoiced and rejuvenated and filled the veins and nerves with threads of ice and fire: it was terrifying.

"Canterbury twenty years ago," said Miss Anning, as one lays a shade over an intense light, or covers some burning peach with a green leaf, for it is too strong, too ripe, too full.

Sometimes she wished she had married. Sometimes the cool peace of middle life, with its automatic devices for shielding mind and body from bruises, seemed to her, compared with the thunder and the livid apple blossom of Canterbury, base. She could imagine something different, more like lightning, more intense. She could imagine some physical sensation. She could imagine...

And, strangely enough, for she had never seen him before, her senses, those tentacles which were thrilled and snubbed, now sent no more messages, now lay quiescent, as if she and Mr Serle knew each other so perfectly – were in fact so closely united that they had only to float side by side down this stream.

Of all things, nothing is so strange as human intercourse, she thought, because of its changes, its extraordinary irrationality, her dislike being now nothing short of the most intense and rapturous love, but directly the word "love" occurred to her, she rejected it, thinking again how obscure the mind was, with its very few words for all these astonishing perceptions, these alternations of pain and pleasure. For how did one name this? That is what she felt now – the withdrawal of human affection, Serle's disappearance, and the instant need they were both under to cover up what was so desolating and degrading to human nature that everyone tried to bury it decently from sight, this withdrawal, this violation of trust – and, seeking some decent acknowledged and accepted burial form, she said:

"Of course, whatever they may do, they can't spoil Canterbury."

He smiled; he accepted it; he crossed his knees the other way about. She did her part, he his. So things came to an end. And over them both came instantly that paralysing blankness of feeling, when nothing bursts from the mind, when its walls appear like slate, when vacancy almost hurts and the eyes petrified and fixed see the same spot (a pattern, a coal scuttle) with an exactness which is terrifying, since no emotion, no idea, no impression of any kind comes to change it, to modify it, to embellish it, since the fountains of feeling seem sealed and, as the mind turns rigid, so does the body – stark, statuesque, so that neither Mr

Serle nor Miss Anning could move or speak, and they felt as if an enchanter had freed them, and spring flushed every vein with streams of life, when Mira Cartwright, tapping Mr Serle archly on the shoulder, said:

"I saw you at the *Meistersinger*,* and you cut me. Villain," said Miss Cartwright, "you don't deserve that I should ever speak to you again."

And they could separate.

The Man Who Loved His Kind*

Trotting through Dean's Yard* that afternoon, Prickett Ellis ran straight into Richard Dalloway – or rather, just as they were passing, the covert side glance which each was casting on the other under his hat over his shoulder, broadened and burst into recognition: they had not met for twenty years. They had been at school together. And what was Ellis doing? The Bar? Of course, of course – he had followed the case in the papers. But it was impossible to talk here. Wouldn't he drop in that evening? (They lived in the same old place – just round the corner.) One or two people were coming. Joynson perhaps. "An awful swell now," said Richard.

"Good – till this evening then," said Richard, and went his way, "jolly glad" (that was quite true) to have met that queer chap, who hadn't changed one bit since he had been at school – just the same knobbly, chubby little boy then, with prejudices sticking out all over him, but uncommonly brilliant: won the Newcastle.* Well – off he went.

Prickett Ellis, however, as he turned and looked at Dalloway disappearing, wished now he had not met him – or, at least, for he had always liked him personally, hadn't promised to come to this party. Dalloway was married, gave parties – wasn't his sort at all. He would have to dress. However, as the evening drew on, he supposed, as he had said that and didn't want to be rude, he must go there.

But what an appalling entertainment! There was Joynson – they had nothing to say to each other. He had been a pompous little boy... he had grown rather more self-important – that was all; there wasn't a single other soul in the room that Prickett Ellis knew. Not one. So, as he could not go at once, without saying a word to Dalloway,

39

who seemed altogether taken up with his duties, bustling about in a white waistcoat, there he had to stand. It was the sort of thing that made his gorge rise. Think of grown-up, responsible men and women doing this every night of their lives! The lines deepened on his blue-and-red shaven cheeks, as he leant against the wall in complete silence, for though he worked like a horse, he kept himself fit by exercise – and he looked hard and fierce, as if his moustaches were dipped in frost. He bristled; he grated. His meagre dress clothes made him look unkempt, insignificant, angular.

Idle, chattering, overdressed, without an idea in their heads, these fine ladies and gentlemen went on talking and laughing – and Prickett Ellis watched them and compared them with the Brunners, who, when they won their case against Fenners' Brewery and got two hundred pounds compensation (it was not half what they should have got), went and spent five of it on a clock for him. That was a decent sort of thing to do – that was the sort of thing that moved one – and he glared more severely than ever at these people, overdressed, cynical, prosperous, and compared what he felt now with what he felt at eleven o'clock that morning when old Brunner and Mrs Brunner in their best clothes, awfully respectable and clean-looking old people, had called in to give him that small token, as the old man put it, standing perfectly upright to make his speech of gratitude and respect for the very able way in which you conducted our case, and Mrs Brunner piped up how it was all due to him, they felt. And they deeply appreciated his generosity – because of course he hadn't taken a fee.

And as he took the clock and put it on the middle of his mantelpiece, he had felt that he wished nobody to see his face. That was what he worked for – that was his reward – and he looked at the people who were actually before his eyes as if they danced over that scene in his chambers and were exposed by it, and as it faded (the Brunners faded), there remained, as if left of that scene, himself, confronting this hostile population, a perfectly plain, unsophisticated man, a man of the people (he straightened himself), very badly dressed, glaring, with not an air or a grace about him, a man who was an ill hand at concealing his feelings, a plain man, an ordinary human being, pitted against the evil, the corruption, the heartlessness of society. But he would not go on staring. Now he put on his spectacles and examined the pictures. He read the titles on a line of books – for the most part poetry. He would have liked well enough to read some of his old favourites again – Shakespeare, Dickens… he wished he ever had time to turn into the National Gallery, but he couldn't – no, one could not. Really one could not – with the world in the state it was in. Not when people all day long wanted your help, fairly clamoured for help. This wasn't an age for luxuries. And he looked at the armchairs and the paper knives and the well-bound books, and shook his head, knowing that he would never have the time, never he was glad to think have the heart, to afford himself such luxuries. The people here would be shocked if they knew what he paid for his tobacco – how he had borrowed his clothes. His one and only extravagance was his little yacht on the Norfolk Broads. And that he did allow himself. He did like once a year to get right away from everybody and lie once a year on his back in a field. He thought how shocked they would be, these fine folk, if they realized the amount of pleasure he got from what he was old-fashioned enough to call "a love of nature" – trees and fields he had known ever since he was a boy.

These fine people would be shocked. Indeed, standing there, putting his spectacles away in his pocket, he felt himself grow more and more shocking every instant. And it was a very disagreeable feeling. He did not feel this – that he loved humanity, that he paid only fivepence an ounce for tobacco and loved nature – naturally and quietly. Each of these pleasures had been turned into a protest. He felt that these people whom he despised made him stand and deliver and justify himself. "I am an ordinary man," he kept saying. And what he said next he was really ashamed of saying, but he said it. "I have done more for my kind in one day than the rest of you in all your lives." Indeed, he could not help himself: he kept recalling scene after scene, like that when the Brunners gave him the clock – he kept reminding himself of the nice things people had said of his humanity, of his generosity, how he had helped them. He kept seeing himself as the wise and tolerant servant of humanity. And he wished he could repeat his praises aloud. It was unpleasant that the sense of his goodness should boil within him. It was still more unpleasant that he could tell no one what people had said about him. Thank the Lord, he kept saying, I shall be back at work tomorrow – and yet he was no longer satisfied simply to slip through the door and go home. He must stay, he must stay until he had justified himself. But how could he? In all that room full of people, he did not know a soul to speak to.

At last Richard Dalloway came up.

"I want to introduce Miss O'Keefe," he said. Miss O'Keefe looked him full in the eyes. She was a rather arrogant, abrupt-mannered woman in the thirties.

Miss O'Keefe wanted an ice or something to drink. And the reason why she asked Prickett Ellis to give it her in what he felt a haughty, unjustifiable manner, was that she had seen a woman and two children, very poor, very tired, pressing against the railings of a square, peering in, that hot afternoon. Can't they be let in? she had thought, her pity rising like a wave, her indignation boiling. No, she rebuked herself the next moment, roughly, as if she boxed her own ears. The whole force of the world can't do it. So she picked up the tennis ball and hurled it back. The whole force of the world can't do it, she said in a fury, and that was why she said so commandingly, to the unknown man:

"Give me an ice."

Long before she had eaten it, Prickett Ellis, standing beside her without taking anything, told her that he had not been to a party for fifteen years; told her that his dress suit was lent him by his brother-in-law; told her that he did not like this sort of thing, and it would have eased him greatly to go on to say that he was a plain man who happened to have a liking for ordinary people, and then would have told her (and been ashamed of it afterwards) about the Brunners and the clock, but she said:

"Have you seen *The Tempest*?"*

Then (for he had not seen *The Tempest*), had he read some book? Again no, and then, putting her ice down, did he ever read poetry?

And Prickett Ellis, feeling something rise within him which would decapitate this young woman, make a victim of her, massacre her, made her sit down there, where they would not be interrupted, on two chairs, in the empty garden, for everyone was upstairs, only you could hear a buzz and a hum and a chatter and a jingle, like the mad accompaniment of some phantom orchestra to a cat or two slinking across the grass, and the wavering of leaves, and the yellow and red fruit like Chinese lanterns wobbling this way and that – the talk seemed like a frantic skeleton dance music set to something very real, and full of suffering.

"How beautiful!" said Miss O'Keefe.

Oh, it was beautiful, this little patch of grass, with the towers of Westminster massed round it black high in the air, after the drawing room; it was silent, after that noise. After all, they had that – the tired woman, the children.

Prickett Ellis lit a pipe. That would shock her; he filled it with shag tobacco – fivepence halfpenny an ounce. He thought how he would lie in his boat smoking – he could see himself, alone, at night, smoking under the stars. For always tonight he kept thinking how he would look if these people here were to see him. He said to Miss O'Keefe, striking a match on the sole of his boot, that he couldn't see anything particularly beautiful out here.

"Perhaps," said Miss O'Keefe, "you don't care for beauty." (He had told her that he had not seen *The Tempest*, that he had not read a book; he looked ill kempt, all moustache, chin and silver watch chain.) She thought nobody need pay a penny for this: the museums are free and the National Gallery – and the country. Of course she knew the objections: the washing, cooking, children – but the root of things, what they were all afraid of saying, was that happiness is dirt-cheap. You can have it for nothing. Beauty.

Then Prickett Ellis let her have it – this pale, abrupt, arrogant woman. He told her, puffing his shag tobacco, what he had done that day. Up at six; interviews; smelling a drain in a filthy slum; then to court.

Here he hesitated, wishing to tell her something of his own doings. Suppressing that, he was all the more caustic. He said it made him sick to hear well-fed, well-dressed women (she twitched her lips, for she was thin, and her dress not up to standard) talk of beauty.

"Beauty!" he said. He was afraid he did not understand beauty apart from human beings.

So they glared into the empty garden, where the lights were swaying and one cat hesitating in the middle, its paw lifted.

Beauty apart from human beings? What did he mean by that? she demanded suddenly.

Well this: getting more and more wrought up, he told her the story of the Brunners and the clock, not concealing his pride in it. That was beautiful, he said.

She had no words to specify the horror his story roused in her. First his conceit, then his indecency in talking about human feelings – it was a blasphemy: no one in the whole world ought to tell a story to prove that they had loved their kind. Yet, as he told it – how the old man had stood up and made his speech – tears came into her eyes... ah, if anyone had ever said that to her! But then again, she felt how it was just this that condemned humanity for ever – never would they reach beyond affecting scenes with clocks; Brunners making speeches to Prickett Ellises. And the Prickett Ellises would always say how they had loved their kind – they would always be lazy, compromising and afraid of beauty. Hence sprung revolutions, from laziness and fear and this love of affecting scenes. Still this man got pleasure from his Brunners, and she was condemned to suffer for ever and ever from her poor women shut out from squares. So they sat silent. Both were very unhappy. For Prickett Ellis was not in the least solaced by what he had said – instead of picking her thorn out, he had rubbed it in; his happiness of the morning had been ruined. Miss O'Keefe was muddled and annoyed; she was muddy instead of clear.

"I'm afraid I am one of those very ordinary people," he said, getting up, "who love their kind."

Upon which Miss O'Keefe almost shouted, "So do I."

Hating each other, hating the whole houseful of people who had given them this painful, this disillusioning evening, these two lovers of their kind got up and without a word parted for ever.

A Summing-Up*

Since it had grown hot and crowded indoors, since there could be no danger on a night like this of damp, since the Chinese lanterns seemed hung red and green fruit in the depths of an enchanted forest, Mr Bertram Pritchard led Mrs Latham into the garden.

The open air and the sense of being out of doors bewildered Sasha Latham, the tall, handsome, rather indolent-looking lady whose majesty of presence was so great that people never credited her with feeling perfectly inadequate and gauche when she had to say something at a party. But so it was, and she was glad that she was with Bertram, who could be trusted, even out of doors, to talk without stopping. Written down what he said was in itself insignificant, but there was no connection between the different remarks. Indeed, if one had taken a pencil and written down his very words – and one night of his talk would have filled a whole book – no one could doubt, reading them, that the poor man was intellectually deficient. This was far from the case, for Mr Pritchard was an esteemed civil servant and a Companion of the Bath, but what was even stranger was that he was almost invariably liked. There was a sound in his voice, some accent or emphasis, some lustre in the incongruity of his ideas, some emanation from his round chubby brown face and robin redbreast's figure, something immaterial and unseizable, which existed and flourished and made itself felt independently of his words – indeed, often in opposition to them. This Sasha Latham would be thinking while he chattered on about his tour in Devonshire, about inns and landladies, about Eddie and Freddie, about cows and night travelling, about cream and stars, about Continental railways and Bradshaw,* catching cod, catching cold, influenza, rheumatism and Keats – she was thinking of him in the abstract as a person whose existence was

46

good, creating him as he spoke in a guise that was different from what he said, and was certainly the true Bertram Pritchard, even though one could not prove it. How could one prove that he was a loyal friend and very sympathetic and... but here, as so often happened talking to Bertram Pritchard, she forgot his existence and began to think of something else.

It was the night she thought of, hitching herself together in some way, taking a look up into the sky. It was the country she smelt suddenly, the sombre stillness of fields under the stars, but here, in Mrs Dalloway's back garden, in Westminster, the beauty, country born and bred as she was, thrilled her because of the contrast presumably; there the smell of hay in the air and behind her the rooms full of people. She walked with Bertram; she walked rather like a stag, with a little give of the ankles, fanning herself, majestic, silent, with all her senses roused, her ears pricked, snuffing the air, as if she had been some wild, but perfectly controlled creature taking its pleasure by night.

This, she thought, is the greatest of marvels – the supreme achievement of the human race. Where there were osier beds and coracles paddling through a swamp, there is this – and she thought of the dry, thick, well-built house, stored with valuables, humming with people coming close to each other, going away from each other, exchanging their views, stimulating each other. And Clarissa Dalloway had made it open in the wastes of the night, had laid paving stones over the bog, and, when they came to the end of the garden (it was in fact extremely small) and she and Bertram sat down on deckchairs, she looked at the house veneratingly, enthusiastically, as if a golden shaft ran through her, and tears formed on it and fell, in profound thanksgiving. Shy though she was and almost incapable when suddenly presented to someone of saying anything, fundamentally humble, she cherished a profound admiration for other people. To be them would be marvellous, but she was condemned to be herself and could only in this silent enthusiastic way, sitting outside in a garden, applaud the society of humanity from which she was excluded. Tags of poetry in praise of them rose to her lips; they were adorable and good – above all courageous, triumphers over night and fens, the survivors, the company of adventurers who, set about with dangers, sail on.

By some malice of fate she was unable to join, but she could sit and praise while Bertram chattered on, he being among the voyagers, as cabin boy or common seaman – someone who ran up masts, gaily whistling. Thinking thus, the branch of some tree in front of her became soaked and steeped in her admiration for the people of the house, dripped gold, or stood sentinel erect. It was part of the gallant and carousing company – a mast from which the flag streamed. There was a barrel of some kind against the wall, and this too she endowed.

Suddenly Bertram, who was restless physically, wanted to explore the grounds, and, jumping onto a heap of bricks, he peered over the garden wall. Sasha peered over too. She saw a bucket, or perhaps a boot. In a second the illusion vanished. There was London again; the vast inattentive impersonal world; motor omnibuses; affairs; lights before public houses; and yawning policemen.

Having satisfied his curiosity and replenished, by a moment's silence, his bubbling fountains of talk, Bertram invited Mr and Mrs Somebody to sit with them, pulling up two more chairs. There they sat again, looking at the same house, the same tree, the same barrel – only, having looked over the wall and had a glimpse of the bucket, or rather of London going its ways unconcernedly, Sasha could no longer spray over the world that cloud of gold. Bertram talked and the somebodies – for the life of her she could not remember if they were called Wallace or Freeman – answered, and all their words passed through a thin haze of gold and fell into prosaic daylight. She looked at the dry thick Queen Anne house; she did her best to remember what she had read at school about the Isle of Thorney* and men in coracles, oysters and wild duck and mists, but it seemed to her a logical affair of drains and carpenters, and this party… nothing but people in evening dress.

Then she asked herself: which view is the true one? She could see the bucket and the house half lit up, half unlit.

She asked this question of that somebody whom, in her humble way, she had composed out of the wisdom and power of other people. The answer came often by accident – she had known her old spaniel answer her by wagging his tail.

Now the tree, denuded of its gilt and majesty, seemed to supply her with an answer, became a field tree – the only one in a marsh. She had often seen it – seen the red-flushed clouds between its branches or the moon split up, darting irregular flashes of silver. But what answer? Well, that the soul – for she was conscious of a movement in her of some creature beating its way about her and trying to escape, which momentarily she called the soul – is by nature unmated, a widow bird, a bird perched aloof on that tree.

But then Bertram, putting his arm through hers in his familiar way, for he had known her all her life, remarked that they were not doing their duty and must go in.

At that moment, in some backstreet or public house, the usual terrible, sexless, inarticulate voice rang out – a shriek, a cry. And the widow bird, startled, flew away, descrying wider and wider circles until it became (what she called her soul) remote as a crow which has been startled up into the air by a stone thrown at it.*

A Woman's College from Outside*

The feathery-white moon never let the sky grow dark; all night the chestnut blossoms were white in the green, and dim was the cow parsley in the meadows.* Neither to Tartary nor to Arabia went the wind of the Cambridge courts, but lapsed dreamily in the midst of grey-blue clouds over the roofs of Newnham.* There, in the garden, if she needed space to wander, she might find it among the trees – and as none but women's faces could meet her face, she might unveil it blank, featureless, and gaze into rooms where at that hour, blank, featureless, eyelids white over eyes, ringless hands extended upon sheets, slept innumerable women. But here and there a light still burned.

A double light one might figure in Angela's room, seeing how bright Angela herself was, and how bright came back the reflection of herself from the square glass. The whole of her was perfectly delineated – perhaps the soul. For the glass held up an untrembling image – white and gold, red slippers, pale hair with blue stones in it, and never a ripple or shadow to break the smooth kiss of Angela and her reflection in the glass, as if she were glad to be Angela. Anyhow, the moment was glad – the bright picture hung in the heart of night, the shrine hollowed in the nocturnal blackness. Strange indeed to have this visible proof of the rightness of things: this lily floating flawless upon Time's pool, fearless, as if this were sufficient – this reflection. Which meditation she betrayed by turning, and the mirror held nothing at all, or only the brass bedstead, and she, running here and there, patting and darting, became like a woman in a house, and changed again, pursing her lips over a black book and marking with her finger what surely could not be a firm grasp of the science of economics. Only, Angela Williams was at Newnham for the purpose of earning her living, and could not forget even in moments of impassioned adoration the cheques of her father at Swansea; her mother washing in the scullery; pink frocks out to dry on the line – tokens that even the lily no longer floats flawless upon the pool, but has a name on a card like another.

A. Williams – one may read it in the moonlight, and next to it some Mary or Eleanor, Mildred, Sarah, Phoebe upon square cards on their doors. All names, nothing but names. The cool white light withered them and starched them until it seemed as if the only purpose of all these names was to rise martially in order should there be a call on them to extinguish a fire, suppress an insurrection or pass an examination. Such is the power of names written upon cards pinned upon doors. Such too the resemblance, what with tiles, corridors and bedroom doors, to dairy or nunnery, a place of seclusion or discipline, where the bowl of milk stands cool and pure and there's a great washing of linen.

At that very moment soft laughter came from behind a door. A prim-voiced clock struck the hour – one, two. Now, if the clock were issuing his commands, they were disregarded. Fire, insurrection, examination were all snowed under by laughter or softly uprooted, the sound seeming to bubble up from the depths and gently waft away the hour, rules, discipline. The bed was strewn with cards. Sally was on the floor. Helena in the chair. Good Bertha clasping her hands by the fireplace. A. Williams came in yawning.

"Because it's utterly and intolerably damnable," said Helena.

"Damnable," echoed Bertha. Then yawned.

"We're not eunuchs."

"I saw her slipping in by the back gate with that old hat on. They don't want us to know."

"They?" said Angela. "She."

Then the laughter.

The cards were spread, falling with their red-and-yellow faces on the table, and hands were dabbled in the cards. Good Bertha, leaning with her head against the chair, sighed profoundly. For she would willingly have slept, but since night is free pasturage, a limitless field, since night is unmoulded richness, one must tunnel into its darkness. One must hang it with jewels. Night was shared in secret, day browsed on by the whole flock. The blinds were up. A mist was on the garden. Sitting on the floor by the window (while the others played), body, mind, both together, seemed blown through the air, to trail across the bushes. Ah, but she desired to stretch out in bed and to sleep! She believed that no one felt her desire for sleep; she believed humbly – sleepily, with sudden nods and lurchings – that other people were wide awake. When they laughed all together, a bird chirped in its sleep out in the garden, as if the laughter...

Yes, as if the laughter (for she dozed now) floated out much like mist and attached itself by soft elastic shreds to plants and bushes, so that the garden was vaporous and clouded. And then, swept by the wind, the bushes would bow themselves and the white vapour blow off across the world.

From all the rooms where women slept this vapour issued, attaching itself to shrubs, like mist, and then blew freely out into the open. Elderly women slept who would, on waking, immediately clasp the ivory rod of office. Now smooth and colourless, reposing deeply, they lay surrounded, lay supported, by the bodies of youth recumbent or grouped at the window; pouring forth into the garden this bubbling laughter, this irresponsible laughter – this laughter of mind and body floating away rules, hours, discipline, immensely fertilizing, yet formless, chaotic, trailing and straying and tufting the rose bushes with shreds of vapour.

"Ah," breathed Angela, standing at the window in her nightgown. Pain was in her voice. She leant her head out. The mist was cleft as if her voice parted it. She had been talking, while the others played, to Alice Avery, about Bamburgh Castle;* the colour of the sands at evening – upon which Alice said she would write and settle the day, in August, and, stooping, kissed her, at least touched her head with her hand, and Angela, positively unable to sit still, like one possessed of a wind-lashed sea in her heart, roamed up and down the room (the witness of such a scene), throwing her arms out to relieve this excitement, this astonishment at the incredible stooping of the miraculous tree with the golden fruit at its summit: hadn't it dropped into her arms? She held it glowing to her breast, a thing not to be touched, thought of or spoken about, but left to glow there. And then, slowly putting there her stockings, there her slippers, folding her petticoat neatly on top, Angela, her other name being Williams, realized – how could she express it? – that after the dark churning of myriad ages here was light at the end of the tunnel: life, the world. Beneath her it lay – all good, all lovable. Such was her discovery.

Indeed, how could one then feel surprise if, lying in bed, she could not close her eyes – something irresistibly unclosed them – if in the shallow darkness chair and chest of drawers looked stately and the looking glass precious with its ashen hint of day? Sucking her thumb like a child (her age nineteen last November), she lay in this good world, this new world, this world at the end of the tunnel, until a desire to see it or forestall it drove her, tossing her blankets, to guide herself to the window – and there, looking out upon the garden, where the mist lay, all the windows open, one fiery-bluish, something murmuring in the distance, the world of course, and the morning coming, "Oh," she cried, as if in pain.

The New Dress*

Mabel had her first serious suspicion that something was wrong as she took her cloak off and Mrs Barnet, while handing her the mirror and touching the brushes and thus drawing her attention, perhaps rather markedly, to all the appliances for tidying and improving hair, complexion, clothes, which existed on the dressing table, confirmed the suspicion: that it was not right, not quite right – which growing stronger as she went upstairs and springing at her with conviction as she greeted Clarissa Dalloway, she went straight to the far end of the room, to a shaded corner where a looking glass hung and looked. No! It was not *right*. And at once the misery which she always tried to hide, the profound dissatisfaction – the sense she had had, ever since she was a child, of being inferior to other people – set upon her, relentlessly, remorselessly, with an intensity which she could not beat off, as she would when she woke at night at home, by reading Borrow or Scott,* for oh these men, oh these women, all were thinking: "What's Mabel wearing? What a fright she looks! What a hideous new dress!" – their eyelids flickering as they came up and then their lids shutting rather tight. It was her own appalling inadequacy; her cowardice; her mean, water-sprinkled blood that depressed her. And at once the whole of the room where, for ever so many hours, she had planned with the little dressmaker how it was to go, seemed sordid, repulsive, and her own drawing room so shabby, and herself, going out, puffed up with vanity as she touched the letters on the hall table and said "How dull!" to show off – all this now seemed unutterably silly, paltry and provincial. All this had been absolutely destroyed, shown up, exploded, the moment she came into Mrs Dalloway's drawing room.

What she had thought that evening when, sitting over the teacups, Mrs Dalloway's invitation came was that, of course, she could not be fashionable. It was absurd to pretend it even – fashion meant cut, meant style, meant thirty guineas* at least – but why not be original? Why not be herself, anyhow? And, getting up, she had taken that old fashion book of her mother's, a Paris fashion book of the time of the Empire,* and had thought how much prettier, more dignified and more womanly they were then, and so set herself – oh, it was foolish – trying to be like them, pluming herself in fact, upon being modest and old-fashioned, and very charming, giving herself up, no doubt about it, to an orgy of self-love, which deserved to be chastised, and so rigged herself out like this.

But she dared not look in the glass. She could not face the whole horror – the pale-yellow, idiotically old-fashioned silk dress with its long skirt and its high sleeves and its waist and all the things that looked so charming in the fashion book, but not on her, not among all these ordinary people. She felt like a dressmaker's dummy standing there, for young people to stick pins into.

"But, my dear, it's perfectly charming!" Rose Shaw said, looking her up and down with that little satirical pucker of the lips which she expected – Rose herself being dressed in the height of fashion, precisely like everybody else, always.

We are all like flies trying to crawl over the edge of the saucer,* Mabel thought, and repeated the phrase as if she were crossing herself, as if she were trying to find some spell to annul this pain, to make this agony endurable. Tags of Shakespeare, lines from books she had read ages ago, suddenly came to her when she was in agony, and she repeated them over and over again. "Flies trying to crawl," she repeated. If she could say that over often enough and make herself see the flies, she would become numb, chill, frozen, dumb. Now she could see flies crawling slowly out of a saucer of milk with their wings stuck together, and she strained and strained (standing in front of the looking glass, listening to Rose Shaw) to make herself see Rose Shaw and all the other people there as flies, trying to hoist themselves out of something or into something – meagre, insignificant, toiling flies. But she could not see them like that, not other people. She saw herself like that – she was a fly, but the others were dragonflies, butterflies, beautiful insects, dancing, fluttering, skimming, while she alone dragged herself up out of the saucer. (Envy and spite, the most detestable of the vices, were her chief faults.)

"I feel like some dowdy, decrepit, horribly dingy old fly," she said, making Robert Haydon stop just to hear her say that, just to reassure herself by furbishing up a poor weak-kneed phrase and so showing how detached she was, how witty, that she did not feel in the least out of anything. And, of course, Robert Haydon answered something quite polite, quite insincere, which she saw through instantly, and said to herself, directly he went (again from some book), "Lies, lies, lies!"* For a party makes things either much more real or much less real, she thought; she saw in a flash to the bottom of Robert Haydon's heart; she saw through everything. She saw the truth. *This* was true, this drawing room, this self, the other false. Miss Milan's little workroom was really terribly hot, stuffy, sordid. It smelt of clothes and cabbage cooking – and yet when Miss Milan put the glass in her hand and she looked at herself with the dress on, finished, an extraordinary bliss shot through her heart. Suffused with light, she sprang into existence. Rid of cares and wrinkles, what she had dreamt of herself was there – a beautiful woman. Just for a second (she had not dared look longer: Miss Milan wanted to know about the length of the skirt), there looked at her, framed in the scrolloping* mahogany, a grey-white, mysteriously smiling, charming girl, the core of herself, the soul of herself – and it was not vanity only, not only self-love that made her think it good, tender and true. Miss Milan said the skirt could not well be longer – if anything, the skirt, said Miss Milan, puckering her forehead, considering with all her wits about her, must be shorter – and she felt, suddenly, honestly, full of love for Miss Milan, much, much fonder of Miss Milan than of anyone in the whole world, and could have cried for pity that she should be crawling on the floor with her mouth full of pins, and her face red and her eyes bulging... that one human being should be doing this for another – and she saw them all as human beings merely, and herself going off to her party, and Miss Milan pulling the cover over the canary's cage, or letting him pick a hemp seed from between her lips, and the thought of it, of this side of human nature and its patience and its endurance and its being content with such miserable, scanty, sordid little pleasures filled her eyes with tears.

And now the whole thing had vanished. The dress, the room, the love, the pity, the scrolloping looking glass and the canary's cage – all had vanished, and here she was in a corner of Mrs Dalloway's drawing room, suffering tortures, woken wide awake to reality.

But it was all so paltry, weak-blooded and petty-minded to care so much at her age, with two children, to be still so utterly dependent on people's opinions and not have principles or convictions, not to be able to say, as other people did, "There's Shakespeare! There's death! We're all weevils in a captain's biscuit"* – or whatever it was that people did say.

She faced herself straight in the glass; she pecked at her left shoulder; she issued out into the room as if spears were thrown at her yellow dress from all sides. But instead of looking fierce or tragic, as Rose Shaw would have done (Rose would have looked like Boadicea),* she looked foolish and self-conscious, and simpered like a schoolgirl and slouched across the room, positively slinking, as if she were a beaten mongrel, and looked at a picture, an engraving. As if one went to a party to look at a picture! Everybody knew why she did it: it was from shame, from humiliation.

"Now the fly's in the saucer," she said to herself, "right in the middle, and can't get out – and the milk," she thought, rigidly staring at the picture, "is sticking its wings together."

"It's so old-fashioned," she said to Charles Burt, making him stop (which by itself he hated) on his way to talk to someone else.

She meant, or she tried to make herself think that she meant, that it was the picture and not her dress that was old-fashioned.

And one word of praise, one word of affection from Charles would have made all the difference to her at the moment. If he had only said "Mabel, you're looking charming tonight!", it would have changed her life. But then she ought to have been truthful and direct. Charles said nothing of the kind, of course. He was malice itself. He always saw through one, especially if one were feeling particularly mean, paltry or feeble-minded.

"Mabel's got a new dress!" he said, and the poor fly was absolutely shoved into the middle of the saucer. Really, he would like her to drown, she believed. He had no heart, no fundamental kindness, only a veneer of friendliness. Miss Milan was much more real, much kinder. If only one could feel that and stick to it, always. "Why," she asked herself – replying to Charles much too pertly, letting him see that she was out of temper, or "ruffled", as he called it ("Rather ruffled?" he said, and went on to laugh at her with some woman over there) – "Why," she asked herself, "can't I feel one thing always, feel quite sure that Miss Milan is right and Charles wrong and stick to it, feel sure about the canary and pity and love and not be whipped all round in a second by coming into a room full of people?" It was her odious, weak, vacillating character again, always giving at the critical moment and not being seriously interested in conchology, etymology, botany, archaeology, cutting up potatoes and watching them fructify like Mary Dennis, like Violet Searle.

Then Mrs Holman, seeing her standing there, bore down upon her. Of course a thing like a dress was beneath Mrs Holman's notice, with her family always tumbling downstairs or having the scarlet fever. Could Mabel tell her if Elmthorpe was ever let for August and September? Oh, it was a conversation that bored her unutterably! – it made her furious to be treated like a house agent or a messenger boy, to be made use of. Not to have value, that was it, she thought, trying to grasp something hard, something real, while she tried to answer sensibly about the bathroom and the south aspect and the hot water to the top of the house – and all the time she could see little bits of her yellow dress in the round looking glass, which made them all the size of boot buttons or tadpoles, and it was amazing to think how much humiliation and agony and self-loathing and effort and passionate ups and downs of feeling were contained in a thing the size of a threepenny bit.* And what was still odder, this thing, this Mabel Waring, was separate, quite disconnected – and though Mrs Holman (the black button) was leaning forward and telling her how her eldest boy had strained his heart running, she could see her, too, quite detached in the looking glass, and it was impossible that the black dot, leaning forward, gesticulating, should make the yellow dot, sitting solitary, self-centred, feel what the black dot was feeling, yet they pretended.

"So impossible to keep boys quiet" – that was the kind of thing one said.

And Mrs Holman, who could never get enough sympathy and snatched what little there was greedily, as if it were her right (but she deserved much more, for there was her little girl who had come down this morning with a swollen knee joint), took this miserable offering and looked at it suspiciously, grudgingly, as if it were a halfpenny when it ought to have been a pound, and put it away in her purse, must put up with it, mean and miserly though it was, times being hard, so very hard – and on she went, creaking, injured Mrs Holman, about the girl with the swollen joints. Ah, it was tragic, this greed, this clamour of human beings, like a row of cormorants* barking and flapping their wings for sympathy – it was tragic, could one have felt it and not merely pretended to feel it!

But in her yellow dress tonight she could not wring out one drop more; she wanted it all, all for herself. She knew (she kept on looking into the glass, dipping into that dreadfully showing-up blue pool) that she was condemned, despised, left like this in a backwater, because of her being like this, a feeble, vacillating creature – and it seemed to her that the yellow dress was a penance which she had deserved, and if she had been dressed like Rose Shaw, in lovely, clinging green with a ruffle of swansdown, she would have deserved that, and she thought that there was no escape for her – none whatever. But it was not her fault altogether, after all. It was being one of a family of ten, never having money enough, always skimping and paring, and her mother carrying great cans, and the linoleum worn on the stair edges, and one sordid little domestic tragedy after another (nothing catastrophic: the sheep farm failing, but not utterly; her eldest brother marrying beneath him, but not very much) – there was no romance, nothing extreme about them all. They petered out respectably in seaside resorts; every watering place had one of her aunts even now asleep in some lodging with the front windows not quite facing the sea. That was so like them – they had to squint at things always. And she had done the same – she was just like her aunts. For all her dreams of living in India, married to some hero like Sir Henry Lawrence,* some empire builder (still the sight of a native in a turban filled her with romance), she had failed utterly. She had married Hubert, with his safe, permanent underling's job in the Law Courts,* and they managed tolerably in a small-ish house, without proper maids, and hash when she was alone or just bread and butter, but now and then – Mrs Holman was off, thinking her the most dried-up, unsympathetic twig she had ever met... absurdly dressed, too, and would tell everyone about Mabel's fantastic appearance – now and then, thought Mabel Waring, left alone on the blue sofa, punching the cushion in order to look occupied, for she would not join Charles Burt and Rose Shaw, chattering like magpies and perhaps laughing at her by the fireplace, now and then there did come to her delicious moments: reading the other night in bed, for instance, or down by the sea on the sand in the sun, at Easter – let her recall it – a great tuft of pale sand grass standing all twisted like a shock of spears against the sky, which was blue like a smooth china egg, so firm, so hard, and then the melody of the waves... "Hush, hush," they said, and the children's shouts paddling – yes, it was a divine moment, and there she lay, she felt, in the hand of the goddess who was the world, rather a hard-hearted but very beautiful goddess, a little lamb laid on the altar (one did think these silly things, and it didn't matter so long as one never said them). And also with Hubert sometimes she had quite unexpectedly – carving the mutton for Sunday lunch, for no reason, opening a letter, coming into a room – divine moments, when she said to herself (for she would never say this to anybody else), "This is it. This has happened. This is it!" And the other way about it was equally surprising – that is, when everything was arranged: music, weather, holidays, every reason for happiness was there – then nothing happened at all. One wasn't happy. It was flat, just flat, that was all.

Her wretched self again, no doubt! She had always been a fretful, weak, unsatisfactory mother, a wobbly wife, lolling about in a kind of twilight existence with nothing very clear or very bold or more one thing than another, like all her brothers and sisters, except perhaps Herbert – they were all the same: poor water-veined creatures who did nothing. Then in the midst of this creeping, crawling life, suddenly she was on the crest of a wave. That wretched fly – where had she read the story that kept coming into her mind about the fly and the saucer? – struggled out. Yes, she had those moments. But now that she was forty, they might come more and more seldom. By degrees she would cease to struggle any more. But that was deplorable! That was not to be endured! That made her feel ashamed of herself!

She would go to the London Library tomorrow. She would find some wonderful, helpful, astonishing book, quite by chance, a book by a clergyman, by an American no one had ever heard of – or she would walk down the Strand and drop, accidentally, into a hall where a miner was telling about the life in the pit and suddenly she would become a new person. She would be absolutely transformed. She would wear a uniform; she would be called Sister Somebody; she would never give a thought to clothes again. And for ever after she would be perfectly clear about Charles Burt and Miss Milan and this room and that room – and it would be always, day after day, as if she were lying in the sun or carving the mutton. It would be it!

So she got up from the blue sofa, and the yellow button in the looking glass got up too, and she waved her hand to Charles and Rose to show them she did not depend on them one scrap, and the yellow button moved out of the looking glass, and all the spears were gathered into her breast as she walked towards Mrs Dalloway and said, "Goodnight."

"But it's too early to go," said Mrs Dalloway, who was always so charming.

"I'm afraid I must," said Mabel Waring. "But," she added in her weak, wobbly voice, which only sounded ridiculous when she tried to strengthen it, "I have enjoyed myself enormously."

"I have enjoyed myself," she said to Mr Dalloway, whom she met on the stairs.

"Lies, lies, lies!" she said to herself, going downstairs, and "Right in the saucer!" she said to herself as she thanked Mrs Barnet for helping her and wrapped herself, round and round and round, in the Chinese cloak she had worn these twenty years.

"Slater's Pins Have No Points"*

"Slater's pins have no points – don't you always find that?" said
Miss Craye, turning round as the rose fell out of Fanny Wilmot's
dress, and Fanny stooped with her ears full of the music, to look
for the pin on the floor.

The words gave her an extraordinary shock, as Miss Craye struck
the last chord of the Bach fugue. Did Miss Craye actually go to
Slater's and buy pins then, Fanny Wilmot asked herself, transfixed
for a moment? Did she stand at the counter waiting like anybody
else, and was she given a bill with coppers wrapped in it, and did
she slip them into her purse and then, an hour later, stand by her
dressing table and take out the pins? What need had she of pins?
For she was not so much dressed as cased, like a beetle compactly in
its sheath, blue in winter, green in summer. What need had she of
pins – Julia Craye – who lived, it seemed, in the cool glassy world of
Bach fugues, playing to herself what she liked and only consenting
to take one or two pupils at the Archer Street College of Music (so
the principal, Miss Kingston, said) as a special favour to herself,
who had "the greatest admiration for her in every way". Miss
Craye was left badly off, Miss Kingston was afraid, at her brother's
death. Oh, they used to have such lovely things, when they lived
at Salisbury... and her brother Julius was, of course, a very well-
known man, a famous archaeologist. It was a great privilege to stay
with them, Miss Kingston said ("My family had always known
them – they were regular Salisbury people," Miss Kingston said),
but a little frightening for a child: one had to be careful not to slam
the door or bounce into the room unexpectedly. Miss Kingston,
who gave little character sketches like this on the first day of term
while she received cheques and wrote out receipts for them, smiled
here. Yes, she had been rather a tomboy; she had bounced in and

set all those green Roman glasses and things jumping in their case. The Crayes were none of them married. The Crayes were not used to children. They kept cats. The cats, one used to feel, knew as much about the Roman urns and things as anybody.

"Far more than I did!" said Miss Kingston brightly, writing her name across the stamp in her dashing, cheerful, full-bodied hand, for she had always been practical.

Perhaps then, Fanny Wilmot thought, looking for the pin, Miss Craye said that about "Slater's pins having no points" at a venture. None of the Crayes had ever married. She knew nothing about pins – nothing whatever. But she wanted to break the spell that had fallen on the house – to break the pane of glass which separated them from other people. When Polly Kingston, that merry little girl, had slammed the door and made the Roman vases jump, Julius, seeing that no harm was done (that would be his first instinct) looked, for the case was stood in the window, at Polly skipping home across the fields, looked with the look his sister often had – that lingering, desiring look.

"Stars, sun, moon," it seemed to say, "the daisy in the grass, fires, frost on the window pane, my heart goes out to you. But," it always seemed to add, "you break, you pass, you go." And simultaneously it covered the intensity of both these states of mind with "I can't reach you – I can't get at you", spoken wistfully, frustratedly. And the stars faded, and the child went.

That was the kind of spell, that was the glassy surface that Miss Craye wanted to break by showing, when she had played Bach beautifully as a reward to a favourite pupil (Fanny Wilmot knew that she was Miss Craye's favourite pupil), that she too felt as other people felt about pins. Slater's pins had no points.

Yes, the "famous archaeologist" had looked like that too. "The famous archaeologist" – as she said that, endorsing cheques, ascertaining the day of the month, speaking so brightly and frankly, there was in Miss Kingston's voice an indescribable tone which hinted at something odd, something queer, in Julius Craye. It was the very same thing that was odd perhaps in Julia too.

One could have sworn, thought Fanny Wilmot, as she looked for the pin, that at parties, meetings (Miss Kingston's father was a clergyman), she had picked up some piece of gossip, or it might only have been a smile, or a tone when his name was mentioned, which had given her "a feeling" about Julius Craye. Needless to say, she had never spoken about it to anybody. Probably she scarcely knew what she meant by it. But whenever she spoke of Julius or heard him mentioned, that was the first thought that came to mind: there was something odd about Julius Craye.

It was so that Julia looked too as she sat half-turned on the music stool, smiling. It's on the field, it's on the pane, it's in the sky – beauty – and I can't get at it, I can't have it... I, she seemed to add, with that little clutch of the hand which was so characteristic, who adore it so passionately, would give the whole world to possess it! And she picked up the carnation which had fallen on the floor, while Fanny searched for the pin. She crushed it, Fanny felt, voluptuously in her smooth, veined hands stuck about with water-coloured rings set in pearls. The pressure of her fingers seemed to increase all that was most brilliant in the flower, to set it off, to make it more frilled, fresh, immaculate. What was odd in her, and perhaps in her brother too, was that this crush and grasp of the fingers was combined with a perpetual frustration. So it was even now with the carnation. She had her hands on it – she pressed it – but she did not possess it, enjoy it, not altogether.

None of the Crayes had married, Fanny Wilmot remembered. She had in mind how one evening, when the lesson had lasted longer than usual and it was dark, Julia Craye had said "It's the use of men, surely, to protect us", smiling at her that same odd smile, as she stood fastening her cloak, which made her, like the flower, conscious to her fingertips of youth and brilliance, but, like the flower too, Fanny suspected, inhibited.

"Oh, but I don't want protection," Fanny had laughed, and when Julia Craye, fixing on her that extraordinary look, had said she was not so sure of that, Fanny positively blushed under the admiration in her eyes.

It was the only use of men, she had said. Was it for that reason then, Fanny wondered, with her eyes on the floor, that she had never married? After all, she had not lived all her life in Salisbury. "Much the nicest part of London," she had said once, "(but I'm speaking of fifteen or twenty years ago) is Kensington. One was in the Gardens in ten minutes – it was like the heart of the country. One could dine out in one's slippers without catching cold. Kensington... it was like a village then, you know," she had said.

Here she had broken off, to denounce acridly the draughts in the Tubes.*

"It was the use of men," she had said, with a queer, wry acerbity. Did that throw any light on the problem why she had not married? One could imagine every sort of scene in her youth, when with her good blue eyes, her straight firm nose, her piano playing, her rose flowering with chaste passion in the bosom of her muslin dress, she had attracted first the young men to whom such things – and the china teacups and the silver candlesticks, and the inlaid tables (for the Crayes had such nice things) – were wonderful, young men not sufficiently distinguished, young men of the cathedral town with ambitions. She had attracted them first, and then her brother's friends from Oxford or Cambridge. They would come down in the summer, row her up the river, continue the argument about Browning* by letter, and arrange perhaps, on the rare occasions when she stayed in London, to show her... Kensington Gardens?

"Much the nicest part of London... Kensington. I'm speaking of fifteen or twenty years ago," she had said once. "One was in the Gardens in ten minutes – in the heart of the country." One could make that yield what one liked, Fanny Wilmot thought, single out for instance Mr Sherman, the painter, an old friend of hers; make him call for her by appointment one sunny day in June; take her to have tea under the trees. (They had met, too, at those parties to which one tripped in slippers without fear of catching cold.) The aunt or other elderly relative was to wait there while they looked at the Serpentine.* They looked at the Serpentine. He may have rowed her across. They compared it with the Avon. She would have considered the comparison very seriously, for views of rivers were important to her. She sat hunched a little, a little angular, though she was graceful then, steering. At the critical moment, for he had determined that he must speak now – it was his only chance of getting her alone – he was speaking with his head turned at an absurd angle, in his great nervousness, over his shoulder... at that very moment she interrupted fiercely. He would have them into the bridge, she cried. It was a moment of horror, of disillusionment, of revelation for both of them. I can't have it, I can't possess it, she thought. He could not see why she had come, then. With a great splash of his oar he pulled the boat round. Merely to snub him? He rowed her back and said goodbye to her.

The setting of that scene could be varied as one chose, Fanny Wilmot reflected. (Where had that pin fallen?) It might be Ravenna – or Edinburgh, where she had kept house for her brother. The scene could be changed, and the young man and the exact manner of it all, but one thing was constant: her refusal and her frown and her anger with herself afterwards, and her argument, and her relief – yes, certainly her immense relief. The very next day perhaps she would get up at six, put on her cloak and walk all the way from Kensington to the river. She was so thankful that she had not sacrificed her right to go and look at things when they are at their best – before people are up, that is to say. She could have her breakfast in bed, if she liked. She had not sacrificed her independence.

Yes, Fanny Wilmot smiled, Julia had not endangered her habits. They remained safe, and her habits would have suffered if she had married. "They're ogres," she had said one evening, half laughing, when another pupil, a girl lately married, suddenly bethinking her that she would miss her husband, had rushed off in haste.

"They're ogres," she had said, laughing grimly. An ogre would have interfered perhaps with breakfast in bed, with walks at dawn down to the river. What would have happened (but one could hardly conceive this) had she had children? She took astonishing precautions against chills, fatigue, rich food, the wrong food, draughts, heated rooms, journeys in the Tube, for she could never determine which of these it was exactly that brought on those terrible headaches that gave her life the semblance of a battlefield. She was always engaged in outwitting the enemy, until it seemed as if the pursuit had its interest – could she have beaten the enemy finally, she would have found life a little dull. As it was, the tug of war was perpetual – on one side, the nightingale or the view which she loved with passion (yes, for views and birds she felt nothing less than passion), on the other, the damp path or the horrid long drag up a steep hill which would certainly make her good for nothing next day and bring on one of her headaches. When, therefore, from time to time, she managed her forces adroitly and brought off a visit to Hampton Court the week the crocuses (those glossy bright flowers were her favourites) were at their best, it was a victory. It was something that lasted, something that mattered for ever. She strung the afternoon on the necklace of memorable days, which was not too long for her to be able to recall this one or that one – this view, that city – to finger it, to feel it, to savour, sighing, the quality that made it unique.

"It was so beautiful last Friday," she said, "that I determined I must go there." So she had gone off to Waterloo on her great undertaking – to visit Hampton Court – alone. Naturally, but perhaps foolishly, one pitied her for the thing she never asked pity for (indeed she was reticent habitually, speaking of her health only as a warrior might speak of his foe) – one pitied her for always doing everything alone. Her brother was dead. Her sister was asthmatic. She found the climate of Edinburgh good for her. It was too bleak for Julia. Perhaps too she found the associations painful, for her brother, the famous archaeologist, had died there, and she had loved her brother. She lived in a little house off the Brompton Road* entirely alone.

Fanny Wilmot saw the pin on the carpet; she picked it up. She looked at Miss Craye. Was Miss Craye so lonely? No, Miss Craye was steadily, blissfully, if only for a moment, a happy woman. Fanny had surprised her in a moment of ecstasy. She sat there, half turned away from the piano, with her hands clasped in her lap holding the carnation upright, while behind her was the sharp square of the window, uncurtained, purple in the evening, intensely purple after the brilliant electric lights which burned unshaded in the bare music room. Julia Craye sitting hunched and compact holding her flower seemed to emerge out of the London night, seemed to fling it like a cloak behind her. It seemed, in its bareness and intensity, the effluence of her spirit, something she had made which surrounded her, which was her. Fanny stared.

All seemed transparent for a moment to the gaze of Fanny Wilmot, as if, looking through Miss Craye, she saw the very fountain of her being spurt up in pure silver drops. She saw back and back into the past behind her. She saw the green Roman vases stood in their case; heard the choristers playing cricket; saw Julia quietly descend the curving steps onto the lawn; saw her pour out tea beneath the cedar tree; softly enclose the old man's hand in hers; saw her going round and about the corridors of that ancient cathedral dwelling place with towels in her hand to mark them; lamenting as she went the pettiness of daily life; and slowly ageing, and putting away clothes when summer came, because at her age they were too bright to wear; and tending her father's sickness; and cleaving her way ever more definitely as her will stiffened towards her solitary goal; travelling frugally; counting the cost and measuring out of her tight-shut purse the sum needed for this journey or for that old mirror; obstinately adhering whatever people might say in choosing her pleasures for herself. She saw Julia…

She saw Julia open her arms; saw her blaze; saw her kindle. Out of the night she burned like a dead white star. Julia kissed her. Julia possessed her.

"Slater's pins have no points," Miss Craye said, laughing queerly and relaxing her arms as Fanny Wilmot pinned the flower to her breast with trembling fingers.

Three Pictures*

The First Picture

It is impossible that one should not see pictures, because if my
father was a blacksmith and yours was a peer of the realm, we
must needs be pictures to each other. We cannot possibly break
out of the frame of the picture by speaking natural words. You
see me leaning against the door of the smithy with a horseshoe
in my hand and you think, as you go by: "How picturesque!" I,
seeing you sitting so much at your ease in the car, almost as if you
were going to bow to the populace, think: "What a picture of old,
luxurious, aristocratical England!" We both are quite wrong in
our judgements no doubt, but that is inevitable.

So now, at the turn of the road, I saw one of these pictures. It
might have been called *The Sailor's Homecoming*, or some such
title. A fine young sailor carrying a bundle; a girl with her hand
on his arm; neighbours gathering round; a cottage garden ablaze
with flowers; as one passed, one read at the bottom of that picture
that the sailor was back from China, and there was a fine spread
waiting for him in the parlour, and he had a present for his young
wife in his bundle, and she was soon going to bear him their first
child. Everything was right and good and as it should be, one
felt about that picture. There was something wholesome and
satisfactory in the sight of such happiness: life seemed sweeter
and more enviable than before.

So thinking I passed them, filling in the picture as fully, as
completely as I could, noticing the colour of her dress, of his eyes,
seeing the sandy cat slinking round the cottage door.

For some time the picture floated in my eyes, making most
things appear much brighter, warmer and simpler than usual,

and making some things appear foolish, and some things wrong and some things right, and more full of meaning than before. At odd moments during that day and the next, the picture returned to one's mind, and one thought with envy, but with kindness, of the happy sailor and his wife; one wondered what they were doing, what they were saying now. The imagination supplied other pictures springing from that first one, a picture of the sailor cutting firewood, drawing water, and they talked about China, and the girl set his present on the chimney piece, where everyone who came could see it, and she sewed at her baby clothes, and all the doors and windows were open into the garden so that the birds were flittering and the bees humming, and Rogers – that was his name – could not say how much to his liking all this was after the China seas. As he smoked his pipe, with his foot in the garden.

The Second Picture

In the middle of the night a loud cry rang through the village. Then there was a sound of something scuffling, and then dead silence. All that could be seen out of the window was the branch of lilac tree hanging motionless and ponderous across the road. It was a hot, still night. There was no moon. The cry made everything seem ominous. Who had cried? Why had she cried? It was a woman's voice, made by some extremity of feeling almost sexless, almost expressionless. It was as if human nature had cried out against some iniquity, some inexpressible horror. There was dead silence. The stars shone perfectly steadily. The fields lay still. The trees were motionless. Yet all seemed guilty, convicted, ominous. One felt that something ought to be done. Some light ought to appear tossing, moving agitatedly. Someone ought to come running down the road. There should be lights in the cottage windows. And then perhaps another cry, but less sexless, less wordless, comforted, appeased. But no light came. No feet were heard. There was no second cry. The first had been swallowed up, and there was dead silence.

One lay in the dark listening intently. It had been merely a voice. There was nothing to connect it with. No picture of any sort came to interpret it, to make it intelligible to the mind. But as the dark arose at last, all one saw was an obscure human form, almost without shape, raising a gigantic arm in vain against some overwhelming iniquity.

The Third Picture

The fine weather remained unbroken. Had it not been for that single cry in the night, one would have felt that the earth had put into harbour; that life had ceased to drive before the wind; that it had reached some quiet cove and there lay anchored, hardly moving, on the quiet waters. But the sound persisted. Wherever one went – it might be for a long walk up into the hills – something seemed to turn uneasily beneath the surface, making the peace, the stability all round one seem a little unreal. There were the sheep clustered on the side of the hill; the valley broke in long tapering waves like the fall of smooth waters. One came on solitary farmhouses. The puppy rolled in the yard. The butterflies gambolled over the gorse. All was as quiet, as safe as could be. Yet, one kept thinking, a cry had rent it – all this beauty had been an accomplice that night, had consented to remain calm, to be still beautiful; at any moment it might be sundered again. This goodness, this safety were only on the surface.

And then, to cheer oneself out of this apprehensive mood, one turned to the picture of the sailor's homecoming. One saw it all over again producing various little details – the blue colour of her dress, the shadow that fell from the yellow-flowering tree – that one had not used before. So they had stood at the cottage door, he with his bundle on his back, she just lightly touching his sleeve with her hand. And a sandy cat had slunk round the door. Thus gradually going over the picture in every detail, one persuaded oneself by degrees that it was far more likely that this calm and content and goodwill lay beneath the surface than anything treacherous, sinister. The sheep grazing, the waves of the valley, the farmhouse, the puppy, the dancing butterflies were in fact like that all through. And so one turned back home, with one's mind fixed on the sailor and his wife, making up picture after picture of them so that one picture after another of happiness and satisfaction might be laid over that unrest, that hideous cry, until it was crushed and silenced by their pressure out of existence.

Here at last was the village, and the churchyard through which one must pass – and the usual thought came, as one entered it, of the peacefulness of the place, with its shady yews, its rubbed tombstones, its nameless graves. Death is cheerful here, one felt. Indeed, look at that picture! A man was digging a grave, and children were picnicking at the side of it while he worked. As the shovels of yellow earth were thrown up, the children were sprawling about eating bread and jam and drinking milk out of large mugs. The gravedigger's wife, a fat fair woman, had propped herself against a tombstone and spread her apron on the grass by the open grave to serve as a tea table. Some lumps of clay had fallen among the tea things. Who was going to be buried? I asked. Had old Mr Dodson died at last? "Oh! no. It's for young Rogers, the sailor," the woman answered, staring at me. "He died two nights ago, of some foreign fever. Didn't you hear his wife? She rushed into the road and cried out... Here, Tommy, you're all covered with earth!"

What a picture it made!

The Lady in the Looking Glass:
A Reflection*

People should not leave looking glasses hanging in their rooms any more than they should leave open chequebooks or letters confessing some hideous crime. One could not help looking, that summer afternoon, in the long glass that hung outside in the hall. Chance had so arranged it. From the depths of the sofa in the drawing room one could see reflected in the Italian glass not only the marble-topped table opposite, but a stretch of the garden beyond. One could see a long grass path leading between banks of tall flowers until, slicing off an angle, the gold rim cut it off.

The house was empty, and one felt, since one was the only person in the drawing room, like one of those naturalists who, covered with grass and leaves, lie watching the shyest animals – badgers, otters, kingfishers – moving about freely, themselves unseen. The room that afternoon was full of such shy creatures, lights and shadows, curtains blowing, petals falling – things that never happen, so it seems, if someone is looking. The quiet old country room with its rugs and stone chimney pieces, its sunken bookcases and red-and-gold lacquer cabinets, was full of such nocturnal creatures. They came pirouetting across the floor, stepping delicately with high-lifted feet and spread tails and pecking allusive beaks as if they had been cranes or flocks of elegant flamingos whose pink was faded, or peacocks whose trains were veined with silver. And there were obscure flushes and darkenings too, as if a cuttlefish had suddenly suffused the air with purple, and the room had its passions and rages and envies and sorrows coming over it and clouding it, like a human being. Nothing stayed the same for two seconds together.

But, outside, the looking glass reflected the hall table, the sunflowers, the garden path so accurately and so fixedly that they seemed held there in their reality unescapably. It was a strange contrast: all changing here, all stillness there. One could not help looking from one to the other. Meanwhile, since all the doors and windows were open in the heat, there was a perpetual sighing and ceasing sound, the voice of the transient and the perishing, it seemed, coming and going like human breath, while in the looking glass things had ceased to breathe and lay still in the trance of immortality.

Half an hour ago the mistress of the house, Isabella Tyson, had gone down the grass path in her thin summer dress, carrying a basket, and had vanished, sliced off by the gilt rim of the looking glass. She had gone presumably into the lower garden to pick flowers – or, as it seemed more natural to suppose, to pick something light and fantastic and leafy and trailing: traveller's joy, or one of those elegant sprays of convolvulus that twine round ugly walls and burst here and there into white and violet blossoms. She suggested the fantastic and the tremulous convolvulus rather than the upright aster, the starched zinnia or her own burning roses, alight like lamps on the straight posts of their rose trees. The comparison showed how very little, after all these years, one knew about her, for it is impossible that any woman of flesh and blood of fifty-five or sixty should be really a wreath or a tendril. Such comparisons are worse than idle and superficial – they are cruel even, for they come like the convolvulus itself trembling between one's eyes and the truth. There must be truth; there must be a wall. Yet it was strange that after knowing her all these years one could not say what the truth about Isabella was; one still made up phrases like this about convolvulus and traveller's joy. As for facts, it was a fact that she was a spinster; that she was rich; that she had bought this house and collected with her own hands – often in the most obscure corners of the world and at great risk from poisonous stings and oriental diseases – the rugs, the chairs, the cabinets which now lived their nocturnal life before one's eyes. Sometimes it seemed as if they knew more about her than we – who sat on them, wrote at them and trod on them so carefully – were allowed to know. In each of these cabinets were many little drawers, and each almost certainly held letters, tied with bows of ribbon, sprinkled with sticks of lavender or rose leaves. For it was another fact (if facts were what one wanted) that Isabella had known many people, had had many friends, and thus, if one had the audacity to open a drawer and read her letters, one would find the traces of many agitations, of appointments to meet, of upbraidings for not having met, long letters of intimacy and affection, violent letters of jealousy and reproach, terrible final words of parting – for all those interviews and assignations had led to nothing (that is, she had never married), and yet, judging from the mask-like indifference of her face, she had gone through twenty times more of passion and experience than those whose loves are trumpeted forth for all the world to hear. Under the stress of thinking about Isabella, her room became more shadowy and symbolic; the corners seemed darker, the legs of chairs and tables more spindly and hieroglyphic.

Suddenly these reflections were ended violently, and yet without a sound. A large black form loomed into the looking glass, blotted out everything, strewed the table with a packet of marble tablets veined with pink and grey and was gone. But the picture was entirely altered. For the moment it was unrecognizable and irrational and entirely out of focus. One could not relate these tablets to any human purpose. And then by degrees some logical process set to work on them and began ordering and arranging them and bringing them into the fold of common experience. One realized at last that they were merely letters. The man had brought the post.

There they lay on the marble-topped table, all dripping with light and colour at first and crude and unabsorbed. And then it was strange to see how they were drawn in and arranged and composed and made part of the picture and granted that stillness and immortality which the looking glass conferred. They lay there invested with a new reality and significance, and with a greater heaviness too, as if it would have needed a chisel to dislodge them from the table. And, whether it was fancy or not, they seemed to have become not merely a handful of casual letters, but to be tablets graven with eternal truth – if one could read them, one would know everything there was to be known about Isabella, yes, and about life too. The pages inside those marble-looking envelopes must be cut deep and scored thick with meaning. Isabella would come in and take them, one by one, very slowly, and open them, and read them carefully word by word, and then with a profound sigh of comprehension, as if she had seen to the bottom of everything, she would tear the envelopes to little bits and tie the letters together and lock the cabinet drawer in her determination to conceal what she did not wish to be known.

The thought served as a challenge. Isabella did not wish to be known – but she should no longer escape. It was absurd, it was monstrous. If she concealed so much and knew so much, one must prise her open with the first tool that came to hand – the imagination. One must fix one's mind upon her at that very moment. One must fasten her down there. One must refuse to be put off any longer with sayings and doings such as the moment brought forth – with dinners and visits and polite conversations. One must put oneself in her shoes. If one took the phrase literally, it was easy to see the shoes in which she stood, down in the lower garden, at this moment. They were very narrow and long and fashionable – they were made of the softest and most flexible leather. Like everything she wore, they were exquisite. And she would be standing under the high hedge in the lower part of the garden, raising the scissors that were tied to her waist to cut some dead flower, some overgrown branch. The sun would beat down on her face, into her eyes – but no, at the critical moment a veil of cloud covered the sun, making the expression of her eyes doubtful: was it mocking or tender, brilliant or dull? One could only see the indeterminate outline of her rather faded, fine face looking at the sky. She was thinking, perhaps, that she must order a new net for the strawberries; that she must send flowers to Johnson's widow;

that it was time she drove over to see the Hippesleys in their new house. Those were the things she talked about at dinner, certainly. But one was tired of the things that she talked about at dinner. It was her profounder state of being that one wanted to catch and turn to words, the state that is to the mind what breathing is to the body, what one calls happiness or unhappiness. At the mention of those words it became obvious, surely, that she must be happy. She was rich; she was distinguished; she had many friends; she travelled – she bought rugs in Turkey and blue pots in Persia. Avenues of pleasure radiated this way and that from where she stood with her scissors raised to cut the trembling branches while the lacy clouds veiled her face.

Here with a quick movement of her scissors she snipped the spray of traveller's joy, and it fell to the ground. As it fell, surely some light came in too, surely one could penetrate a little further into her being. Her mind then was filled with tenderness and regret... To cut an overgrown branch saddened her because it had once lived, and life was dear to her. Yes, and at the same time the fall of the branch would suggest to her how she must die herself and all the futility and evanescence of things. And then again quickly catching this thought up, with her instant good sense, she thought life had treated her well: even if fall she must, it was to lie on the earth and moulder sweetly into the roots of violets. So she stood thinking. Without making any thought precise – for she was one of those reticent people whose minds hold their thoughts enmeshed in clouds of silence – she was filled with thoughts. Her mind was like her room, in which lights advanced and retreated, came pirouetting and stepping delicately, spread their tails, pecked their way – and then her whole being was suffused, like the room again, with a cloud of some profound knowledge, some unspoken regret, and then she was full of locked drawers, stuffed with letters, like her cabinets. To talk of "prising her open" as if she were an oyster, to use any but the finest and subtlest and most pliable tools upon her, was impious and absurd. One must imagine – here was she in the looking glass. It made one start.

She was so far off at first that one could not see her clearly. She came lingering and pausing, here straightening a rose, there lifting a pink to smell it, but she never stopped, and all the time she became larger and larger in the looking glass, more and more completely the person into whose mind one had been trying to penetrate. One verified her by degrees – fitted the qualities one had discovered into this visible body. There were her grey-green dress and her long shoes, her basket and something sparkling at her throat. She came so gradually that she did not seem to derange the pattern in the glass, but only to bring in some new element which gently moved and altered the other objects as if asking them, courteously, to make room for her. And the letters and the table and the grass walk and the sunflowers which had been waiting in the looking glass separated and opened out so that she might be received among them. At last there she was, in the hall. She stopped dead. She stood by the table. She stood perfectly still. At once the looking glass began to pour over her a light that seemed to fix her, that seemed like some acid to bite off the unessential and superficial and to leave only the truth. It was an enthralling spectacle. Everything dropped from her – clouds, dress, basket, diamond – all that one had called the creeper and convolvulus. Here was the hard wall beneath. Here was the woman herself. She stood naked in that pitiless light. And there was nothing. Isabella was perfectly empty. She had no thoughts. She had no friends. She cared for nobody. As for her letters, they were all bills. Look: as she stood there, old and angular, veined and lined, with her high nose and her wrinkled neck, she did not even trouble to open them.

People should not leave looking glasses hanging in their rooms.

The Shooting Party*

I

She got in and put her suitcase in the rack and the brace of pheasants on top of it. Then she sat down in the corner. The train was rattling through the midlands, and the fog, which came in when she opened the door, seemed to enlarge the carriage and set the four travellers apart. Obviously M.M. (those were the initials on the suitcase) had been staying the weekend with a shooting party – obviously, for she was telling over the story now, lying back in her corner. She did not shut her eyes. But clearly she did not see the man opposite, nor the coloured photograph of York Minster. She must have heard, too, what they had been saying. For as she gazed, her lips moved; now and then she smiled. And she was handsome: a cabbage rose, a russet apple, tawny, but scarred on the jaw – the scar lengthened when she smiled. Since she was telling over the story, she must have been a guest there, and yet, dressed as she was, out of fashion as women dressed, years ago, in pictures in fashion plates of sporting newspapers, she did not seem exactly a guest, nor yet a maid. Had she had a basket with her, she would have been the woman who breeds fox terriers, the owner of the Siamese cat, someone connected with hounds and horses. But she had only a suitcase and the pheasants. Somehow therefore she must have wormed her way into the room that she was seeing through the stuffing of the carriage and the man's bald head and the picture of York Minster. And she must have listened to what they were saying, for now, like somebody imitating the noise that someone else makes, she made a little click at the back of her throat: "Chk. Chk." Then she smiled.

II

"Chk," said Miss Antonia, pinching her glasses on her nose. The damp leaves fell across the long windows of the gallery; one or two stuck, fish-shaped, and lay like inlaid brown wood upon the window panes. Then the trees in the park shivered, and the leaves, flaunting down, seemed to make the shiver visible – the damp brown shiver.

"Chk," Miss Antonia sniffed again, and pecked at the flimsy white stuff that she held in her hands as a hen pecks nervously, rapidly at a piece of white bread.

The wind sighed. The room was draughty. The doors did not fit, nor the windows. Now and then a ripple, like a reptile, ran under the carpet. On the carpet lay panels of green and yellow, where the sun rested, and then the sun moved and pointed a finger as if in mockery at a hole in the carpet and stopped. And then on it went, the sun's feeble but impartial finger, and lay upon the coat of arms over the fireplace, gently illumined the shield, the pendant grapes, the mermaid and the spears. Miss Antonia looked up as the light strengthened. Vast lands, so they said, the old people had owned – her forefathers, the Rashleighs. Over there. Up the Amazons. Freebooter. Voyagers. Sacks of emeralds. Nosing round the islands. Taking captives. Maidens. There she was, all scales from the tail to the waist. Miss Antonia grinned. Down struck the finger of the sun, and her eye went with it. Now it rested on a silver frame, on a photograph, on an egg-shaped baldish head, on a lip that stuck out under the moustache, and the name "Edward" written with a flourish beneath.

"The King…" Miss Antonia muttered, turning the film of white upon her knee, "had the Blue Room," she added with a toss of her head. The light faded.

Out in the King's Ride the pheasants were being driven across the noses of the guns. Up they spurted from the underwood like heavy rockets, reddish-purple rockets, and, as they rose, the guns cracked in order, eagerly, sharply, as if a line of dogs had suddenly barked. Tufts of white smoke held together for a moment, then gently solved themselves, faded and dispersed.

In the deep-cut road beneath the hanger a cart stood, laid already with soft warm bodies, with limp claws and still-lustrous eyes. The birds seemed alive still, but swooning under their rich damp feathers. They looked relaxed and comfortable, stirring slightly, as if they slept upon a warm bank of soft feathers on the floor of the cart.

Then the squire, with the hangdog, purple-stained face, in the shabby gaiters, cursed and raised his gun.

Miss Antonia stitched on. Now and then a tongue of flame reached round the grey log that stretched from one bar to another across the grate, ate it greedily, then died out, leaving a white bracelet where the bark had been eaten off. Miss Antonia looked up for a moment, stared wide-eyed, instinctively, as a dog stares at a flame. Then the flame sank, and she stitched again.

Then, silently, the enormously high door opened. Two lean men came in, and drew a table over the hole in the carpet. They went out; they came in. They laid a cloth upon the table. They went out; they came in. They brought a green baize basket of knives and forks, and glasses, and sugar casters, and salt cellars, and bread, and a silver vase with three chrysanthemums in it. And the table was laid. Miss Antonia stitched on.

Again the door opened, pushed feebly this time. A little dog trotted in, a spaniel, nosing nimbly; it paused. The door stood open. And then, leaning on her stick, heavily, old Miss Rashleigh entered. A white shawl, diamond-fastened, clouded her baldness. She hobbled, crossed the room, hunched herself in the high-backed chair by the fireside. Miss Antonia went on stitching.

"Shooting," she said at last.

Old Miss Rashleigh nodded. "In the King's Ride," she said. She gripped her stick. They sat waiting.

The shooters had moved now from the King's Ride to the Home Woods. They stood in the purple ploughed field outside. Now and then a twig snapped; leaves came whirling. But above the mist and the smoke was an island of blue – faint blue, pure blue – alone in the sky. And in the innocent air, as if straying alone like a cherub, a bell from a far hidden steeple frolicked, gambolled, then faded. Then again up shot the rockets, the reddish-purple pheasants. Up and up they went. Again the guns barked; the smoke balls formed, loosened, dispersed. And the busy little dogs ran nosing nimbly over the fields, and the warm damp bodies, still languid and soft, as if in a swoon, were bunched together by the men in gaiters and flung into the cart.

"There!" grunted Milly Masters, the housekeeper, throwing down her glasses. She was stitching too in the small dark room that overlooked the stable yard. The jersey, the rough woollen jersey for her son, the boy who cleaned the church, was finished. "The end o' that!" she muttered. Then she heard the cart. Wheels ground on the cobbles. Up she got. With her hands to her hair, her chestnut-coloured hair, she stood in the yard, in the wind.

"Coming!" she laughed, and the scar on her cheek lengthened. She unbolted the door of the game room as Wing, the keeper, drove the cart over the cobbles. The birds were dead now, their claws gripped tight, though they gripped nothing. The leathery eyelids were creased greyly over their eyes. Mrs Masters the housekeeper, Wing the gamekeeper, took bunches of dead birds by the neck and flung them down on the slate floor of the game larder. The slate floor became smeared and spotted with blood. The pheasants looked smaller now, as if their bodies had shrunk together. Then Wing lifted the tail of the cart and drove in the pins which secured it. The sides of the cart were stuck about with little grey-blue feathers, and the floor was smeared and stained with blood. But it was empty.

"The last of the lot!" Milly Masters grinned as the cart drove off.

"Luncheon is served, ma'am," said the butler. He pointed at the table; he directed the footman. The dish with the silver cover was placed precisely there where he pointed. They waited, the butler and the footman.

Miss Antonia laid her white film upon the basket, put away her silk, her thimble, stuck her needle through a piece of flannel and hung her glasses on a hook upon her breast. Then she rose.

"Luncheon!" she barked in old Miss Rashleigh's ear. One second later, old Miss Rashleigh stretched her leg out, gripped her stick and rose too. Both old women advanced slowly to the table, and were tucked in by the butler and the footman, one at this end, one at that. Off came the silver cover. And there was the pheasant, featherless, gleaming, the thighs tightly pressed to its side, and little mounds of breadcrumbs were heaped at either end.

Miss Antonia drew the carving knife across the pheasant's breast firmly. She cut two slices and laid them on a plate. Deftly the footman whipped it from her, and old Miss Rashleigh raised her knife. Shots rang out in the wood under the window.

"Coming?" said old Miss Rashleigh, suspending her fork.

The branches flung and flaunted on the trees in the park.

She took a mouthful of pheasant. Falling leaves flicked the window pane; one or two stuck to the glass.

"In the Home Woods, now," said Miss Antonia. "Hugh's last shoot." She drew her knife down the other side of the breast. She added potatoes and gravy, Brussels sprouts and bread sauce methodically in a circle round the slices on her plate. The butler and the footman stood watching, like servers at a feast. The old ladies ate quietly, silently, nor did they hurry themselves; methodically they cleaned the bird. Bones only were left on their plates. Then the butler drew the decanter towards Miss Antonia and paused for a moment with his head bent.

"Give it here, Griffiths," said Miss Antonia, and took the carcass in her fingers and tossed it to the spaniel beneath the table. The butler and the footman bowed and went out.

"Coming closer," said Miss Rashleigh, listening. The wind was rising. A brown shudder shook the air; leaves flew too fast to stick. The glass rattled in the windows.

"Birds wild," Miss Antonia nodded, watching the helter-skelter. Old Miss Rashleigh filled her glass.* As they sipped, their eyes became lustrous like half-precious stones held to the light. Slate-blue were Miss Rashleigh's; Miss Antonia's red, like port. And their laces and their flounces seemed to quiver, as if their bodies were warm and languid underneath their feathers as they drank.

"It was a day like this, d'you remember?" said old Miss Rashleigh, fingering her glass. "They brought him home... a bullet through his heart. A bramble, so they said. Tripped. Caught his foot..." She chuckled as she sipped her wine.

"And John..." said Miss Antonia. "The mare, they said, put her foot in a hole. Died in the field. The hunt rode over him. He came home, too, on a shutter..." They sipped again.

"Remember Lily?" said old Miss Rashleigh. "A bad 'un." She shook her head. "Riding with a scarlet tassel on her cane..."

"Rotten at the heart!" cried Miss Antonia. "Remember the colonel's letter? 'Your son rode as if he had twenty devils in him – charged at the head of his men...' Then one white devil... ah hah!" She sipped again.

"The men of our house..." began Miss Rashleigh. She raised her glass. She held it high, as if she toasted the mermaid carved in plaster on the fireplace. She paused. The guns were barking. Something cracked in the woodwork. Or was it a rat running behind the plaster?

"Always women..." Miss Antonia nodded. "The men of our house. Pink-and-white Lucy at the Mill – d' you remember?"

"Ellen's daughter at the Goat and Sickle," Miss Rashleigh added.

"And the girl at the tailor's," Miss Antonia murmured, "where Hugh bought his riding breeches, the little dark shop on the right..."

"...that used to be flooded every winter. It's *his* boy," Miss Antonia chuckled, leaning towards her sister, "that cleans the church."

There was a crash. A slate had fallen down the chimney. The great log had snapped in two. Flakes of plaster fell from the shield above the fireplace.

"Falling," old Miss Rashleigh chuckled, "falling."

"And who," said Miss Antonia, looking at the flakes on the carpet, "who's to pay?"

Crowing like old babies, indifferent, reckless, they laughed, crossed to the fireplace and sipped their sherry by the wood ashes and the plaster until each glass held only one drop of wine, reddish-purple, at the bottom. And this the old women did not wish to part with, so it seemed, for they fingered their glasses, as they sat side by side by the ashes, but they never raised them to their lips.

"Milly Masters in the still room," began old Miss Rashleigh. "She's our brother's—"

A shot barked beneath the window. It cut the string that held the rain. Down it poured – down, down, down – in straight rods whipping the windows. Light faded from the carpet. Light faded in their eyes, too, as they sat by the white ashes listening. Their eyes became like pebbles taken from water, grey stones dulled and dried. And their hands gripped their hands like the claws of dead birds gripping nothing. And they shrivelled as if the bodies inside the clothes had shrunk. Then Miss Antonia raised her glass to the mermaid. It was the last toast, the last drop; she drank it off. "Coming!" she croaked, and slapped the glass down. A door banged below. Then another. Then another. Feet could be heard trampling, yet shuffling, along the corridor towards the gallery.

"Closer! Closer!" grinned Miss Rashleigh, baring her three yellow teeth.

The immensely high door burst open. In rushed three great hounds and stood panting. Then there entered, slouching, the squire himself in shabby gaiters. The dogs pressed round him, tossing their heads, snuffling at his pockets. Then they bounded forward. They smelt the meat. The floor of the gallery waved like a wind-lashed forest with the tails and backs of the great questing hounds. They snuffed the table. They pawed the cloth. Then with a wild neighing whimper they flung themselves upon the little yellow spaniel who was gnawing the carcass under the table.

"Curse you, curse you!" howled the squire. But his voice was weak, as if he shouted against a wind. "Curse you, curse you!" he shouted, now cursing his sisters.

Miss Antonia and Miss Rashleigh rose to their feet. The great dogs had seized the spaniel. They worried him, they mauled him with their great yellow teeth. The squire swung a leather-knotted tawse* this way, that way, cursing the dogs, cursing his sisters, in the voice that sounded so loud yet so weak. With one lash he curled to the ground the vase of chrysanthemums. Another caught old Miss Rashleigh on the cheek. The old woman staggered backwards. She fell against the mantelpiece. Her stick, striking wildly, struck the shield above the fireplace. She fell with a thud upon the ashes. The shield of the Rashleighs crashed from the wall. Under the mermaid, under the spears, she lay buried.

The wind lashed the panes of glass; shots volleyed in the park, and a tree fell. And then King Edward in the silver frame slid, toppled and fell too.

III

The grey mist had thickened in the carriage. It hung down like a veil; it seemed to put the four travellers in the corners at a great distance from each other, though in fact they were as close as a third-class railway carriage could bring them. The effect was strange. The handsome, if elderly, the well-dressed, if rather shabby woman who had got into the train at some station in the midlands seemed to have lost her shape. Her body had become all mist. Only her eyes gleamed, changed, lived all by themselves it seemed – eyes without a body, blue-grey eyes seeing something invisible. In the misty air they shone out, they moved, so that in the sepulchral atmosphere – the windows were blurred, the lamps haloed with fog – they were like lights dancing, will-o'-the-wisps that move, people say, over the graves of unquiet sleepers in churchyards. An absurd idea? Mere fancy! Yet after all, since there is nothing that does not leave some residue and memory is a light that dances in the mind when the reality is buried, why should not the eyes there, gleaming, moving, be the ghost of a family, of an age, of a civilization dancing over the grave?

The train slowed down. One after another lamps stood up, held their yellow heads erect for a second, then were felled. Up they stood again as the train slid into the station. The lights massed and blazed. And the eyes in the corner? They were shut; the lids were closed. They saw nothing. Perhaps the light was too strong. And of course in the full blaze of the station lamps it was plain: she was quite an ordinary, rather elderly woman travelling to London on some quite ordinary piece of business – something connected with a cat or a horse or a dog. She reached for her suitcase, rose and took the pheasants from the rack. But did she, all the same, as she opened the carriage door and stepped out, murmur "Chk. Chk" as she passed?

The Duchess and the Jeweller*

Oliver Bacon lived at the top of a house overlooking the Green Park. He had a flat; chairs jutted out at the right angles – chairs covered in hide. Sofas filled the bays of the windows – sofas covered in tapestry. The windows, the three long windows, had the proper allowance of discreet net and figured satin. The mahogany sideboard bulged discreetly with the right brandies, whiskies and liqueurs. And from the middle window he looked down upon the glossy roofs of fashionable cars packed in the narrow straits of Piccadilly. A more central position could not be imagined. And at eight in the morning he would have his breakfast brought in on a tray by a manservant; the manservant would unfold his crimson dressing gown; he would rip his letters open with his long pointed nails and would extract thick white cards of invitation upon which the engraving stood up roughly from duchesses, countesses, viscountesses and Honourable Ladies. Then he would wash; then he would eat his toast; then he would read his paper by the bright burning fire of electric coals.

"Behold Oliver," he would say, addressing himself. "You who began life in a filthy little alley, you who..." And he would look down at his legs, so shapely in their perfect trousers; at his boots; at his spats. They were all shapely, shining, cut from the best cloth by the best scissors in Savile Row. But he dismantled himself often and became again a little boy in a dark alley. He had once thought that the height of his ambition – selling stolen dogs to fashionable women in Whitechapel. And once he had been done. "Oh, Oliver," his mother had wailed. "Oh, Oliver! When will you have sense, my son?"... Then he had gone behind a counter, had sold cheap watches; then he had taken a wallet to Amsterdam... At that memory he would chuckle – the old Oliver remembering the young. Yes, he had done well with the three diamonds; also, there was the commission on the emerald. After that, he went into the private room behind the shop in Hatton Garden – the room with the scales, the safe, the thick magnifying glasses. And then… and then… He chuckled. When he passed through the knots of jewellers in the hot evening who were discussing prices, gold mines, diamonds, reports from South Africa, one of them would lay a finger to the side of his nose and murmur "Hum-m-m" as he passed. It was no more than a murmur, no more than a nudge on the shoulder, a finger on the nose, a buzz that ran through the cluster of jewellers in Hatton Garden on a hot afternoon – oh, many years ago now! But still Oliver felt it purring down his spine, the nudge, the murmur that meant "Look at him – young Oliver, the young jeweller… There he goes." Young he was then. And he dressed better and better – and had first a hansom cab, then a car, and first he went up to the dress circle, then down into the stalls. And he had a villa at Richmond overlooking the river, with trellises of red roses; and Mademoiselle used to pick one every morning and stick it in his buttonhole.

"So," said Oliver Bacon, rising and stretching his legs. "So…"

And he stood beneath the picture of an old lady on the mantel-piece and raised his hands. "I have kept my word," he said, laying his hands together, palm to palm, as if he were doing homage to her. "I have won my bet." That was so: he was the richest jewel-ler in England, but his nose, which was long and flexible, like an elephant's trunk, seemed to say by its curious quiver at the nostrils (but it seemed as if the whole nose quivered, not only the nostrils) that he was not satisfied yet – still smelt something under the ground a little further off. Imagine a giant hog in a pasture rich with truffles: after unearthing this truffle and that, still it smells a bigger, a blacker truffle under the ground further off. So Oliver snuffed always in the rich earth of Mayfair another truffle – a blacker, a bigger, further off.

Now then he straightened the pearl in his tie, cased himself in his smart blue overcoat, took his yellow gloves and his cane, and swayed as he descended the stairs and half snuffed, half sighed through his long sharp nose as he passed out into Piccadilly. For was he not still a sad man, a dissatisfied man, a man who seeks something that is hidden, though he had won his bet?

He swayed slightly as he walked, as the camel at the zoo sways from side to side when it walks along the asphalt paths laden with grocers and their wives eating from paper bags and throwing little bits of silver paper crumpled up onto the path. The camel despises the grocers; the camel is dissatisfied with its lot; the camel sees the blue lake and the fringe of palm trees in front of it. So the great jeweller, the greatest jeweller in the whole world, swung down Piccadilly, perfectly dressed, with his gloves, with his cane (but dissatisfied still), till he reached the dark little shop, that was famous in France, in Germany, in Austria, in Italy and all over America – the dark little shop in the street off Bond Street.

As usual, he strode through the shop without speaking, though the four men – the two old men, Marshall and Spencer, and the two young men, Hammond and Wicks – stood straight behind the counter as he passed and looked at him, envying him. It was only with one finger of the amber-coloured glove, waggling, that he acknowledged their presence. And he went in and shut the door of his private room behind him.

Then he unlocked the grating that barred the window. The cries of Bond Street came in, the purr of the distant traffic. The light from reflectors at the back of the shop struck upwards. One tree waved six green leaves, for it was June. But Mademoiselle had married Mr Pedder of the local brewery – no one stuck roses in his buttonhole now.

"So," he half sighed, half snorted, "so…"

Then he touched a spring in the wall and slowly the panelling slid open, and behind it were the steel safes – five, no, six of them, all of burnished steel. He twisted a key, unlocked one, then another. Each was lined with a pad of deep crimson velvet; in each lay jewels – bracelets, necklaces, rings, tiaras, ducal coronets, loose stones in glass shells, rubies, emeralds, pearls, diamonds. All safe, shining, cool, yet burning, eternally, with their own compressed light.

"Tears!" said Oliver, looking at the pearls.

"Heart's blood!" he said, looking at the rubies.

"Gunpowder!" he continued, rattling the diamonds so that they flashed and blazed.

"Gunpowder enough to blow up Mayfair – sky high, high, high!" He threw his head back and made a sound like a horse neighing as he said it.

The telephone buzzed obsequiously in a low muted voice on his table. He shut the safe.

"In ten minutes," he said. "Not before." And he sat down at his desk and looked at the heads of the Roman emperors that were graved on his sleeve links. And again he dismantled himself and became once more the little boy playing marbles in the alley where they sell stolen dogs on Sunday. He became that wily, astute little boy, with lips like wet cherries. He dabbled his fingers in ropes of tripe; he dipped them in pans of frying fish; he dodged in and out among the crowds. He was slim, lissom, with eyes like licked stones. And now... now... the hands of the clock ticked on. One, two, three, four... The Duchess of Lambourne waited his pleasure; the Duchess of Lambourne, daughter of a hundred earls. She would wait for ten minutes on a chair at the counter. She would wait his pleasure. She would wait till he was ready to see her. He watched the clock in its shagreen case. The hand moved on. With each tick the clock handed him – so it seemed – pâté de foie gras, a glass of champagne, another of fine brandy, a cigar costing one guinea. The clock laid them on the table beside him, as the ten minutes passed. Then he heard soft, slow footsteps approaching, a rustle in the corridor. The door opened. Mr Hammond flattened himself against the wall.

"Her Grace!" he announced.

And he waited there, flattened against the wall.

And Oliver, rising, could hear the rustle of the dress of the duchess as she came down the passage. Then she loomed up, filling the door, filling the room with the aroma, the prestige, the arrogance, the pomp, the pride of all the dukes and duchesses swollen in one wave. And as a wave breaks, she broke, as she sat down, spreading and splashing and falling over Oliver Bacon the great jeweller, covering him with sparkling bright colours – green, rose, violet – and odours, and iridescences, and rays shooting from fingers, nodding from plumes, flashing from silk, for she was very large, very fat, tightly girt in pink taffeta, and past her prime. As a parasol with many flounces, as a peacock with many feathers, shuts its flounces, folds its feathers, so she subsided and shut herself as she sank down in the leather armchair.

"Good morning, Mr Bacon," said the duchess. And she held out her hand, which came through the slit of her white glove. And Oliver bent low as he shook it. And as their hands touched, the link was forged between them once more. They were friends, yet enemies: he was master, she was mistress – each cheated the other, each needed the other, each feared the other, each felt this and knew this every time they touched hands thus in the little back room with the white light outside, and the tree with its six leaves, and the sound of the street in the distance and behind them the safes.

"And today, duchess – what can I do for you today?" said Oliver, very softly.

The duchess opened – her heart, her private heart, gaped wide. And with a sigh, but no words, she took from her bag a long wash-leather pouch – it looked like a lean yellow ferret. And from a slit in the ferret's belly she dropped pearls – ten pearls. They rolled from the slit in the ferret's belly – one, two, three, four – like the eggs of some heavenly bird.

"All that's left me, dear Mr Bacon," she moaned. Five, six, seven – down they rolled, down the slopes of the vast mountainsides that fell between her knees into one narrow valley – the eighth, the ninth and the tenth. There they lay in the glow of the peach-blossom taffeta. Ten pearls.

"From the Appleby cincture," she mourned. "The last... the last of them all."

Oliver stretched out and took one of the pearls between finger and thumb. It was round, it was lustrous. But real was it, or false? Was she lying again? Did she dare?

She laid her plump, padded finger across her lips. "If the duke knew…" she whispered. "Dear Mr Bacon, a bit of bad luck…"

Been gambling again, had she?

"That villain! That sharper!" she hissed.

The man with the chipped cheekbone? A bad 'un. And the duke was straight as a poker, with side whiskers – would cut her off, shut her up down there, if he knew… what I know, thought Oliver, and glanced at the safe.

"Araminta, Daphne, Diana," she moaned. "It's for *them*."

The Ladies Araminta, Daphne, Diana – her daughters. He knew them, adored them. But it was Diana he loved.

"You have all my secrets," she leered. Tears slid, tears fell – tears, like diamonds, collecting powder in the ruts of her cherry-blossom cheeks.

"Old friend," she murmured, "old friend."

"Old friend," he repeated, "old friend," as if he licked the words.

"How much?" he queried.

She covered the pearls with her hand.

"Twenty thousand," she whispered.

But was it real or false, the one he held in his hand? The Appleby cincture – hadn't she sold it already? He would ring for Spencer or Hammond. "Take it and test it," he would say. He stretched to the bell.

"You will come down tomorrow?" she urged, she interrupted. "The Prime Minister… His Royal Highness…" She stopped. "And Diana," she added.

Oliver took his hand off the bell.

He looked past her, at the backs of the houses in Bond Street. But he saw not the houses in Bond Street, but a dimpling river, and trout rising and salmon, and the Prime Minister, and himself too, in white waistcoats – and then, Diana. He looked down at the pearl in his hand. But how could he test it, in the light of the river, in the light of the eyes of Diana? But the eyes of the duchess were on him.

"Twenty thousand," she moaned. "My honour!"

The honour of the mother of Diana! He drew his chequebook towards him; he took out his pen.

"Twenty," he wrote. Then he stopped writing. The eyes of the old woman in the picture were on him – of the old woman, his mother.

"Oliver!" she warned him. "Have sense! Don't be a fool!"

"Oliver!" the duchess entreated – it was "Oliver" now, not "Mr Bacon". "You'll come for a long weekend?"

Alone in the woods with Diana! Riding alone in the woods with Diana!

"Thousand," he wrote, and signed it.

"Here you are," he said.

And there opened all the flounces of the parasol, all the plumes of the peacock, the radiance of the wave, the swords and spears of Agincourt,* as she rose from her chair. And the two old men and the two young men – Spencer and Marshall, Wicks and Hammond – flattened themselves behind the counter envying him as he led her through the shop to the door. And he waggled his yellow glove in their faces, and she held her honour – a cheque for twenty thousand pounds with his signature – quite firmly in her hands.

"Are they false or are they real?" asked Oliver, shutting his private door. There they were, ten pearls on the blotting paper on the table. He took them to the window. He held them under his lens to the light... This, then, was the truffle he had routed out of the earth! Rotten at the centre – rotten at the core!

"Forgive me, oh my mother!" he sighed, raising his hands as if he asked pardon of the old woman in the picture. And again he was a little boy in the alley where they sold dogs on Sunday.

"For," he murmured, laying the palms of his hands together, "it is to be a long weekend."

Lappin and Lapinova*

They were married. The wedding march pealed out. The pigeons
fluttered. Small boys in Eton jackets threw rice – a fox terrier
sauntered across the path, and Ernest Thorburn led his bride to
the car through the small inquisitive crowd of complete strangers
which always collects in London to enjoy other people's happiness
or unhappiness. Certainly he looked handsome and she looked
shy. More rice was thrown, and the car moved off.

That was on Tuesday. Now it was Saturday. Rosalind had still to
get used to the fact that she was Mrs Ernest Thorburn. Perhaps
she never would get used to the fact that she was Mrs Ernest
Anybody, she thought, as she sat in the bow window of the
hotel looking over the lake to the mountains and waited for her
husband to come down to breakfast. Ernest was a difficult name
to get used to. It was not the name she would have chosen. She
would have preferred Timothy, Antony or Peter. He did not look
like Ernest either. The name suggested the Albert Memorial,*
mahogany sideboards, steel engravings of the Prince Consort
with his family – her mother-in-law's dining room in Porchester
Terrace, in short.

But here he was. Thank goodness he did not look like Ernest
– no. But what did he look like? She glanced at him sideways.
Well, when he was eating toast, he looked like a rabbit. Not that
anyone else would have seen a likeness to a creature so diminutive
and timid in this spruce, muscular young man with the straight
nose, the blue eyes and the very firm mouth. But that made it
all the more amusing. His nose twitched very slightly when he
ate. So did her pet rabbit's. She kept watching his nose twitch,
and then she had to explain, when he caught her looking at him,
why she laughed.

"It's because you're like a rabbit, Ernest," she said. "Like a wild rabbit," she added, looking at him. "A hunting rabbit – a king rabbit – a rabbit that makes laws for all the other rabbits."

Ernest had no objection to being that kind of rabbit, and since it amused her to see him twitch his nose – he had never known that his nose twitched – he twitched it on purpose. And she laughed and laughed – and he laughed too, so that the maiden ladies and the fishing man and the Swiss waiter in his greasy black jacket all guessed right: they were very happy. But how long does such happiness last? they asked themselves, and each answered according to his own circumstances.

At lunch time, seated on a clump of heather beside the lake, "Lettuce, rabbit?" said Rosalind, holding out the lettuce that had been provided to eat with the hard-boiled eggs. "Come and take it out of my hand," she added, and he stretched out and nibbled the lettuce and twitched his nose.

"Good rabbit, nice rabbit," she said, patting him, as she used to pat her tame rabbit at home. But that was absurd. He was not a tame rabbit, whatever he was. She turned it into French. "Lapin," she called him. But whatever he was, he was not a French rabbit. He was simply and solely English-born at Porchester Terrace, educated at Rugby, now a clerk in His Majesty's Civil Service. So she tried "Bunny" next, but that was worse. "Bunny" was someone plump and soft and comic – he was thin and hard and serious. Still, his nose twitched. "Lappin," she exclaimed suddenly, and gave a little cry as if she had found the very word she looked for.

"Lappin, Lappin, King Lappin," she repeated. It seemed to suit him exactly: he was not Ernest, he was King Lappin. Why? She did not know.

When there was nothing new to talk about on their long solitary walks – and it rained, as everyone had warned them that it would rain – or when they were sitting over the fire in the evening (for it was cold, and the maiden ladies had gone, and the fishing man, and the waiter only came if you rang the bell for him), she let her fancy play with the story of the Lappin tribe. Under her hands

– she was sewing, he was reading – they became very real, very vivid, very amusing. Ernest put down the paper and helped her. There were the black rabbits and the red; there were the enemy rabbits and the friendly. There were the wood in which they lived and the outlying prairies and the swamp. Above all there was King Lappin, who, far from having only the one trick – that he twitched his nose – became, as the days passed, an animal of the greatest character: Rosalind was always finding new qualities in him. But above all he was a great hunter.

"And what," said Rosalind, on the last day of the honeymoon, "did the king do today?"

In fact they had been climbing all day, and she had worn a blister on her heel, but she did not mean that.

"Today," said Ernest, twitching his nose as he bit the end off his cigar, "he chased a hare." He paused, struck a match and twitched again.

"A woman hare," he added.

"A white hare!" Rosalind exclaimed, as if she had been expecting this. "Rather a small hare – silver-grey, with big bright eyes?"

"Yes," said Ernest, looking at her as she had looked at him, "a smallish animal, with eyes popping out of her head and two little front paws dangling." It was exactly how she sat, with her sewing dangling in her hands – and her eyes, that were so big and bright, were certainly a little prominent.

"Ah, Lapinova," Rosalind murmured.

"Is that what she's called?" said Ernest. "The real Rosalind?" He looked at her. He felt very much in love with her.

"Yes – that's what she's called," said Rosalind. "Lapinova." And before they went to bed that night, it was all settled. He was King Lappin, she was Queen Lapinova. They were the very opposite of each other: he was bold and determined, she wary and undependable. He ruled over the busy world of rabbits; her world was a desolate, mysterious place, which she ranged mostly by moonlight. All the same, their territories touched; they were king and queen.

Thus when they came back from their honeymoon they possessed a private world, inhabited, save for the one white hare, entirely by rabbits. No one guessed that there was such a place, and that of course made it all the more amusing. It made them feel, more even than most young married couples, in league together against the rest of the world. Often they looked slyly at each other when people talked about rabbits and woods and traps and shooting. Or they winked furtively across the table when Aunt Mary said that she could never bear to see a hare in a dish: it looked so like a baby – or when John, Ernest's sporting brother, told them what price rabbits were fetching that autumn in Wiltshire, skins and all. Sometimes, when they wanted a gamekeeper or a poacher or a lord of the manor, they amused themselves by distributing the parts among their friends. Ernest's mother, Mrs Reginald Thorburn, for example, fitted the part of the squire to perfection. But it was all secret – that was the point of it: nobody save themselves knew that such a world existed.

Without that world, how, Rosalind wondered, that winter could she have lived at all? For instance, there was the golden-wedding party, when all the Thorburns assembled at Porchester Terrace to celebrate the fiftieth anniversary of that union which had been so blessed (had it not produced Ernest Thorburn?) and so fruitful (had it not produced nine other sons and daughters into the bargain, many themselves married and also fruitful?). She dreaded that party. But it was inevitable. As she walked upstairs, she felt bitterly that she was an only child, and an orphan at that – a mere drop among all those Thorburns assembled in the great drawing room with the shiny satin wallpaper and the lustrous family portraits. The living Thorburns much resembled the painted, save that instead of painted lips they had real lips, out of which came jokes – jokes about schoolrooms, and how they had pulled the chair from under the governess; jokes about frogs and how they had put them between the virgin sheets of maiden ladies. As for herself, she had never even made an apple-pie bed.* Holding her present in her hand, she advanced towards her mother-in-law, sumptuous in yellow satin, and towards her father-in-law, decorated with a rich yellow carnation. All round them on tables and chairs there were golden tributes – some nestling in cotton wool, others branching resplendent: candlesticks, cigar boxes, chains – each stamped with the goldsmith's proof that it was solid gold, hallmarked, authentic. But her present was only a little pinchbeck box pierced with holes, an old sand caster, an eighteenth-century relic once used to sprinkle sand over wet ink. Rather a senseless present, she felt, in an age of blotting paper – and as she proffered it, she saw in front of her the stubby black handwriting in which her mother-in-law, when they were engaged, had expressed the hope that "My son will make you happy". No, she was not happy. Not at all happy. She looked at Ernest, straight as a ramrod, with a nose like all the noses in the family portraits, a nose that never twitched at all.

Then they went down to dinner. She was half hidden by the great chrysanthemums that curled their red and gold petals into large tight balls. Everything was gold. A gold-edged card with gold initials intertwined recited the list of all the dishes that would be set one after another before them. She dipped her spoon in a plate of clear golden fluid. The raw white fog outside had been turned by the lamps into a golden mesh that blurred the edges of the plates and gave the pineapples a rough golden skin. Only she herself in her white wedding dress peering ahead of her with her prominent eyes seemed insoluble as an icicle.

As the dinner wore on, however, the room grew steamy with heat. Beads of perspiration stood out on the men's foreheads. She felt that her icicle was being turned to water. She was being melted, dispersed, dissolved into nothingness, and would soon faint. Then, through the surge in her head and the din in her ears, she heard a woman's voice exclaim, "But they breed so!"

The Thorburns – yes, they breed so, she echoed, looking at all the round red faces that seemed doubled in the giddiness that overcame her and magnified in the gold mist that enhaloed them. "They breed so." Then John bawled:

"Little devils!... Shoot 'em! Jump on 'em with big boots! That's the only way to deal with 'em... rabbits!"

At that word, that magic word, she revived. Peeping between the chrysanthemums, she saw Ernest's nose twitch. It rippled, it ran with successive twitches. And at that a mysterious catastrophe befell the Thorburns. The golden table became a moor with the gorse in full bloom; the din of voices turned to one peal of lark's laughter ringing down from the sky. It was a blue sky – clouds passed slowly. And they had all been changed – the Thorburns. She looked at her father-in-law, a furtive little man with dyed moustaches. His foible was collecting things – seals, enamel boxes, trifles from eighteenth-century dressing tables – which he hid in the drawers of his study from his wife. Now she saw him as he was: a poacher, stealing off with his coat bulging with pheasants and partridges to drop them stealthily into a three-legged pot in his smoky little cottage. That was her real father-in-law: a poacher. And Celia, the unmarried daughter, who always nosed out other people's secrets, the little things they wished to hide – she was a white ferret with pink eyes and a nose clotted with earth from her horrid underground nosings and pokings. Slung round men's shoulders, in a net, and thrust down a hole – it was a pitiable life, Celia's; it was none of her fault. So she saw Celia. And then she looked at her mother-in-law – whom they dubbed "the squire". Flushed, coarse, a bully – she was all that as she stood returning thanks, but now that Rosalind – that is, Lapinova – saw her, she saw behind her the decayed family mansion, the plaster peeling off the walls, and heard her, with a sob in her voice, giving thanks to her children (who hated her) for a world that had ceased to exist. There was a sudden silence. They all stood with their glasses raised – they all drank, then it was over.

"Oh, King Lappin!" she cried as they went home together in the fog. "If your nose hadn't twitched just at the moment, I should have been trapped!"

"But you're safe," said King Lappin, pressing her paw.

"Quite safe," she answered.

And they drove back through the park, king and queen of the marsh, of the mist and of the gorse-scented moor.

Thus time passed – one year, two years of time. And on a winter's night, which happened by a coincidence to be the anniversary of the golden-wedding party – but Mrs Reginald Thorburn was dead; the house was to let; and there was only a caretaker in residence – Ernest came home from the office. They had a nice little home: half a house above a saddler's shop in South Kensington, not far from the Tube station. It was cold, with fog in the air, and Rosalind was sitting over the fire, sewing.

"What d'you think happened to me today?" she began as soon as he had settled himself down with his legs stretched to the blaze. "I was crossing the stream when—"

"What stream?" Ernest interrupted her.

"The stream at the bottom, where our wood meets the black wood," she explained.

Ernest looked completely blank for a moment.

"What the deuce are you talking about?" he asked.

"My dear Ernest!" she cried in dismay. "King Lappin," she added, dangling her little front paws in the firelight. But his nose did not twitch. Her hands – they turned to hands – clutched the stuff she was holding; her eyes popped half out of her head. It took him five minutes at least to change from Ernest Thorburn to King Lappin – and while she waited, she felt a load on the back of her neck, as if somebody were about to wring it. At last he changed to King Lappin; his nose twitched, and they spent the evening roaming the woods much as usual.

But she slept badly. In the middle of the night she woke, feeling as if something strange had happened to her. She was stiff and cold. At last she turned on the light and looked at Ernest lying beside her. He was sound asleep. He snored. But even though he snored, his nose remained perfectly still. It looked as if it had never twitched at all. Was it possible that he was really Ernest, and that she was really married to Ernest? A vision of her mother-in-law's dining room came before her – and there they sat, she and Ernest, grown old, under the engravings, in front of the sideboard... It was their golden-wedding day. She could not bear it.

"Lappin, King Lappin!" she whispered, and for a moment his nose seemed to twitch of its own accord. But he still slept. "Wake up, Lappin, wake up!" she cried.

Ernest woke, and, seeing her sitting bolt upright beside him, he asked:

"What's the matter?"

"I thought my rabbit was dead!" she whimpered. Ernest was angry.

"Don't talk such rubbish, Rosalind," he said. "Lie down and go to sleep."

He turned over. In another moment he was sound asleep and snoring.

But she could not sleep. She lay curled up on her side of the bed, like a hare in its form. She had turned out the light, but the street lamp lit the ceiling faintly, and the trees outside made a lacy network over it as if there were a shadowy grove on the ceiling in which she wandered, turning, twisting, in and out, round and round, hunting, being hunted, hearing the bay of hounds and horns, flying, escaping... until the maid drew the blinds and brought their early tea.

Next day she could settle to nothing. She seemed to have lost something. She felt as if her body had shrunk: it had grown small, and black and hard. Her joints seemed stiff too, and when she looked in the glass, which she did several times as she wandered about the flat, her eyes seemed to burst out of her head, like currants in a bun. The rooms also seemed to have shrunk. Large pieces of furniture jutted out at odd angles, and she found herself knocking against them. At last she put on her hat and went out. She walked along the Cromwell Road, and every room she passed and peered into seemed to be a dining room where people sat eating under steel engravings, with thick yellow lace curtains and mahogany sideboards. At last she reached the Natural History Museum; she used to like it when she was a child. But the first thing she saw when she went in was a stuffed hare standing on sham snow with pink glass eyes. Somehow it made her shiver all over. Perhaps it would be better when dusk fell. She went home and sat over the fire, without a light, and tried to imagine that she was out alone on a moor, and there was a stream rushing, and beyond the stream a dark wood. But she could get no further than the stream. At last she squatted down on the bank on the wet grass and sat crouched in her chair, with her hands dangling empty and her eyes glazed, like glass eyes, in the firelight. Then there was the crack of a gun... She started as if she had been shot. It was only Ernest turning his key in the door. She waited, trembling. He came in and switched on the light. There he stood, tall, handsome, rubbing his hands that were red with cold.

"Sitting in the dark?" he said.

"Oh, Ernest, Ernest!" she cried, starting up in her chair.

"Well, what's up now?" he asked briskly, warming his hands at the fire.

"It's Lapinova..." she faltered, glancing wildly at him out of her great startled eyes. "She's gone, Ernest. I've lost her!"

Ernest frowned. He pressed his lips tight together. "Oh, that's what's up, is it?" he said, smiling rather grimly at his wife. For ten seconds he stood there, silent, and she waited, feeling hands tightening at the back of her neck.

"Yes," he said at length. "Poor Lapinova..." He straightened his tie at the looking glass over the mantelpiece.

"Caught in a trap," he said, "killed," and sat down and read the newspaper.

So that was the end of that marriage.

The Searchlight*

The mansion of the eighteenth-century earl had been changed in the twentieth century into a club. And it was pleasant, after dining in the great room with the pillars and the chandeliers under a glare of light, to go out onto the balcony overlooking the park. The trees were in full leaf, and had there been a moon, one could have seen the pink-and-cream-coloured cockades on the chestnut trees. But it was a moonless night – very warm, after a fine summer's day.

Mr and Mrs Ivimey's party were drinking coffee and smoking on the balcony. As if to relieve them from the need of talking, to entertain them without any effort on their part, rods of light wheeled across the sky. It was peace then – the air force was practising, searching for enemy aircraft in the sky. After pausing to prod some suspected spot, the light wheeled, like the wings of a windmill, or again like the antennae of some prodigious insect, and revealed here a cadaverous stone front, here a chestnut tree with all its blossoms riding, and then suddenly the light struck straight at the balcony, and for a second a bright disc shone – perhaps it was a mirror in a lady's handbag.

"Look!" Mrs Ivimey exclaimed.

The light passed. They were in darkness again.

"You'll never guess what *that* made me see!" she added. Naturally, they guessed.

"No, no, no," she protested. Nobody could guess: only she knew, only she could know, because she was the great-granddaughter of the man himself. He had told her the story. What story? If they liked, she would try to tell it. There was still time before the play.

"But where do I begin?" she pondered. "In the year 1820?... It must have been about then that my great-grandfather was a boy. I'm not young myself" – no, but she was very well set up and handsome – "and he was a very old man when I was a child – when he told me the story. A very handsome old man," she explained, "with a shock of white hair and blue eyes. He must have been a beautiful boy. But queer... That was only natural – seeing how they lived. The name was Comber. They'd come down in the world. They'd been gentlefolk; they'd owned land up in Yorkshire. But when he was a boy, only the tower was left. The house was nothing but a little farmhouse, standing in the middle of the fields. We saw it ten years ago and went over it. We had to leave the car and walk across the fields. There isn't any road to the house. It stands all alone – the grass grows right up to the gate... there were chickens pecking about, running in and out of the rooms. All gone to rack and ruin. I remember a stone fell from the tower suddenly." She paused. "There they lived," she went on, "the old man, the woman and the boy. She wasn't his wife, or the boy's mother. She was just a farmhand, a girl the old man had taken to live with him when his wife died. Another reason perhaps why nobody visited them – why the whole place was gone to rack and ruin. But I remember a coat of arms over the door – and books, old books, gone mouldy. He taught himself all he knew from books. He read and read, he told me, old books, books with maps hanging out from the pages. He dragged them up to the top of the tower – the rope's still there, and the broken steps. There's a chair still in the window with the bottom fallen out – and the window swinging open, and the panes broken, and a view for miles and miles across the moors."

She paused as if she were up in the tower looking from the window that swung open.

"But we couldn't," she said, "find the telescope." In the dining room behind them the clatter of plates grew louder. But Mrs Ivimey, on the balcony, seemed puzzled, because she could not find the telescope.

"Why a telescope?" someone asked her.

"Why? Because if there hadn't been a telescope," she laughed, "I shouldn't be sitting here now!"

And certainly she was sitting there now, a well-set-up, middle-aged woman, with something blue over her shoulders.

"It must have been there," she resumed, "because, he told me, every night, when the old people had gone to bed, he sat at the window looking through the telescope at the stars. Jupiter, Aldebaran, Cassiopeia." She waved her hand at the stars that were beginning to show over the trees. It was growing darker. And the searchlight seemed brighter, sweeping across the sky, pausing here and there to stare at the stars.

"There they were," she went on, "the stars. And he asked himself, my grandfather, the boy, 'What are they? Why are they? And who am I?' as one does, sitting alone, with no one to talk to, looking at the stars."

She was silent. They all looked at the stars that were coming out in the darkness over the trees. The stars seemed very permanent, very unchanging. The roar of London sank away. A hundred years seemed nothing. They felt that the boy was looking at the stars with them. They seemed to be with him, in the tower, looking out over the moors at the stars.

Then a voice behind them said:

"Right you are. Friday."

They all turned, shifted, felt dropped down onto the balcony again.

"Ah, but there was nobody to say that to him," she murmured. The couple rose and walked away.

"*He* was alone," she resumed. "It was a fine summer's day. A June day. One of those perfect summer days when everything seems to stand still in the heat. There were the chickens pecking in the farmyard, the old horse stamping in the stable, the old man dozing over his glass. The woman scouring pails in the scullery. Perhaps a stone fell from the tower. It seemed as if the day would never end. And he had no one to talk to – nothing whatever to do. The whole world stretched before him. The moor rising and falling, the sky meeting the moor, green and blue, green and blue, for ever and ever."

In the half-light, they could see that Mrs Ivimey was leaning over the balcony, with her chin propped on her hands, as if she were looking out over the moors from the top of a tower.

"Nothing but moor and sky, moor and sky, for ever and ever," she murmured.

Then she made a movement, as if she swung something into position.

"But what did the earth look like through the telescope?" she asked.

She made another quick little movement with her fingers, as if she were twirling something.

"He focused it," she said. "He focused it upon the earth. He focused it upon a dark mass of wood upon the horizon. He focused it so that he could see... each tree... each tree separate... and the birds... rising and falling... and a stem of smoke... there... in the midst of the trees... And then... lower... lower..." (she lowered her eyes) "there was a house... a house among the trees... a farmhouse... every brick showed... and the tubs on either side of the door... with flowers in them, blue, pink, hydrangeas perhaps..." She paused. "And then a girl came out of the house... wearing something blue upon her head... and stood there... feeding birds... pigeons... they came fluttering round her... And then... look... A man... A man! He came round the corner. He seized her in his arms! They kissed... they kissed!"

Mrs Ivimey opened her arms and closed them as if she were kissing someone.

"It was the first time he had seen a man kiss a woman – in his telescope – miles and miles away across the moors!"

She thrust something from her – the telescope, presumably. She sat upright.

"So he ran down the stairs. He ran through the fields. He ran down lanes, out upon the high road, through woods. He ran for miles and miles, and just when the stars were showing above the trees, he reached the house... covered with dust, streaming with sweat..."

She stopped, as if she saw him.

"And then, and then… What did he do then? What did he say? And the girl…" they pressed her.

A shaft of light fell upon Mrs Ivimey, as if someone had focused the lens of a telescope upon her. (It was the air force looking for enemy aircraft.) She had risen. She had something blue on her head. She had raised her hand, as if she stood in a doorway, amazed.

"Oh the girl… She was my…" She hesitated, as if she were about to say "myself". But she remembered, and corrected herself. "She was my great-grandmother," she said.

She turned to look for her cloak. It was on a chair behind her.

"But tell us – what about the other man, the man who came round the corner?" they asked.

"That man? That man," Mrs Ivimey murmured, stooping to fumble with her cloak (the searchlight had left the balcony), "he, I suppose, vanished."

"The light," she added, gathering her things about her, "only falls here and there."

The searchlight had passed on. It was now focused on the plain expanse of Buckingham Palace. And it was time they went on to the play.

The Legacy*

"For Sissy Miller." Gilbert Clandon, taking up the pearl brooch that lay among a litter of rings and brooches on a little table in his wife's drawing room, read the inscription: "For Sissy Miller, with my love."

It was like Angela to have remembered even Sissy Miller, her secretary. Yet how strange it was, Gilbert Clandon thought once more, that she had left everything in such order – a little gift of some sort for every one of her friends. It was as if she had foreseen her death. Yet she had been in perfect health when she left the house that morning, six weeks ago – when she stepped off the kerb in Piccadilly and the car had killed her.

He was waiting for Sissy Miller. He had asked her to come; he owed her, he felt, after all the years she had been with them, this token of consideration. Yes, he went on, as he sat there waiting, it was strange that Angela had left everything in such order. Every friend had been left some little token of her affection. Every ring, every necklace, every little Chinese box – she had a passion for little boxes – had a name on it. And each had some memory for him. This he had given her; this – the enamel dolphin with the ruby eyes – she had pounced upon one day in a backstreet in Venice. He could remember her little cry of delight. To him, of course, she had left nothing in particular, unless it were her diary. Fifteen little volumes, bound in green leather, stood behind him on her writing table. Ever since they were married, she had kept a diary. Some of their very few... he could not call them quarrels, say tiffs... had been about that diary. When he came in and found her writing, she always shut it or put her hand over it. "No, no, no," he could hear her say. "After I'm dead – perhaps." So she had left it him as her legacy. It was the only thing they had not shared when she was alive. But he had always taken it for granted that she would outlive him. If only she had stopped one moment and had thought what she was doing, she would be alive now. But she had stepped straight off the kerb, the driver of the car had said at the inquest. She had given him no chance to pull up... Here the sound of voices in the hall interrupted him.

"Miss Miller, sir," said the maid.

She came in. He had never seen her alone in his life – nor, of course, in tears. She was terribly distressed, and no wonder. Angela had been much more to her than an employer. She had been a friend. To himself, he thought, as he pushed a chair for her and asked her to sit down, she was scarcely distinguishable from any other woman of her kind. There were thousands of Sissy Millers – drab little women in black carrying attaché cases. But Angela, with her genius for sympathy, had discovered all sorts of qualities in Sissy Miller. She was the soul of discretion – so silent, so trustworthy... one could tell her anything, and so on.

Miss Miller could not speak at first. She sat there dabbing her eyes with her pocket handkerchief. Then she made an effort.

"Pardon me, Mr Clandon," she said.

He murmured. Of course he understood. It was only natural. He could guess what his wife had meant to her.

"I've been so happy here," she said, looking round. Her eyes rested on the writing table behind him. It was here they had worked – she and Angela. For Angela had her share of the duties that fall to the lot of a prominent politician's wife. She had been the greatest help to him in his career. He had often seen her and Sissy sitting at that table – Sissy at the typewriter, taking down letters from her dictation. No doubt Miss Miller was thinking of that too. Now all he had to do was to give her the brooch his wife had left her. A rather incongruous gift it seemed. It might have been better to have left her a sum of money, or even the typewriter. But there it was – "For Sissy Miller, with my love." And, taking the brooch, he gave it her with the little speech that he had prepared. He knew, he said, that she would value it. His wife had often worn it...

And she replied, as she took it almost as if she too had prepared a speech, that it would always be a treasured possession… She had, he supposed, other clothes upon which a pearl brooch would not look quite so incongruous. She was wearing the little black coat and skirt that seemed the uniform of her profession. Then he remembered – she was in mourning, of course. She, too, had had her tragedy – a brother, to whom she was devoted, had died only a week or two before Angela. In some accident, was it? He could not remember – only Angela telling him. Angela, with her genius for sympathy, had been terribly upset. Meanwhile, Sissy Miller had risen. She was putting on her gloves. Evidently she felt that she ought not to intrude. But he could not let her go without saying something about her future. What were her plans? Was there any way in which he could help her?

She was gazing at the table, where she had sat at her typewriter, where the diary lay. And, lost in her memories of Angela, she did not at once answer his suggestion that he should help her. She seemed for a moment not to understand. So he repeated:

"What are your plans, Miss Miller?"

"My plans? Oh, that's all right, Mr Clandon," she exclaimed. "Please don't bother yourself about me."

He took her to mean that she was in no need of financial assistance. It would be better, he realized, to make any suggestion of that kind in a letter. All he could do now was to say, as he pressed her hand, "Remember, Miss Miller, if there's any way in which I can help you, it will be a pleasure…" Then he opened the door. For a moment, on the threshold, as if a sudden thought had struck her, she stopped.

"Mr Clandon," she said, looking straight at him for the first time, and for the first time he was struck by the expression, sympathetic yet searching, in her eyes. "If at any time," she continued, "there's anything I can do to help you, remember, I shall feel it, for your wife's sake, a pleasure…"

With that she was gone. Her words and the look that went with them were unexpected. It was almost as if she believed, or hoped, that he would need her. A curious, perhaps a fantastic idea occurred to him as he returned to his chair. Could it be that during all those years when he had scarcely noticed her, she, as the novelists say, had entertained a passion for him? He caught his own reflection in the glass as he passed. He was over fifty, but he could not help admitting that he was still, as the looking glass showed him, a very distinguished-looking man.

"Poor Sissy Miller!" he said, half laughing. How he would have liked to share that joke with his wife! He turned instinctively to her diary. "Gilbert," he read, opening it at random, "looked so wonderful…" It was as if she had answered his question. Of course, she seemed to say, you're very attractive to women. Of course Sissy Miller felt that too. He read on. "How proud I am to be his wife!" And he had always been very proud to be her husband. How often, when they dined out somewhere, he had looked at her across the table and said to himself, "She is the loveliest woman here!" He read on. That first year he had been standing for Parliament. They had toured his constituency. "When Gilbert sat down, the applause was terrific. The whole audience rose and sang: 'For he's a jolly good fellow.' I was quite overcome." He remembered that, too. She had been sitting on the platform beside him. He could still see the glance she cast at him, and how she had tears in her eyes. And then? He turned the pages. They had gone to Venice. He recalled that happy holiday after the election. "We had ices at Florian's."* He smiled – she was still such a child; she loved ices. "Gilbert gave me a most interesting account of the history of Venice. He told me that the Doges…" She had written it all out in her schoolgirl hand. One of the delights of travelling with Angela had been that she was so eager to learn. She was so terribly ignorant, she used to say, as if that were not one of her charms. And then – he opened the next volume – they had come back to London. "I was so anxious to make a good impression. I wore my wedding dress." He could see her now sitting next old Sir Edward, and making a conquest of that formidable old man, his chief. He read on rapidly, filling in scene after scene from her scrappy fragments. "Dined at the House of Commons... To an evening party at the Lovegroves. Did I realize my responsibility, Lady L. asked me, as Gilbert's wife?" Then, as the years passed – he took another volume from the writing table – he had become more and more absorbed in his work. And she, of course, was more often alone... It had been a great grief to her, apparently, that they had had no children. "How I wish," one entry read, "that Gilbert had a son!" Oddly enough, he had never much regretted that himself. Life had been so full, so rich as it was. That year he had been given a minor post in the government. A minor post only, but her comment was: "I am quite certain now that he will be prime minister!" Well, if things had gone differently, it might have been so. He paused here to speculate upon what might have been. Politics was a gamble, he reflected – but the game wasn't over yet. Not at fifty. He cast his eyes rapidly over more pages, full of the little trifles, the insignificant, happy, daily trifles that had made up her life.

He took up another volume and opened it at random. "What a coward I am! I let the chance slip again. But it seemed selfish to bother him with my own affairs, when he has so much to think about. And we so seldom have an evening alone." What was the meaning of that? Oh, here was the explanation – it referred to her work in the East End. "I plucked up courage and talked to Gilbert at last. He was so kind, so good. He made no objection." He remembered that conversation. She had told him that she felt so idle, so useless. She wished to have some work of her own. She wanted to do something – she had blushed so prettily, he remembered, as she said it, sitting in that very chair – to help others. He had bantered her a little. Hadn't she enough to do looking after him, after her home? Still, if it amused her, of course he had no objection. What was it? Some district? Some committee? Only, she must promise not to make herself ill. So it seemed that every Wednesday she went to Whitechapel. He remembered how he hated the clothes she wore on those occasions. But she had taken it very seriously, it seemed. The diary was full of references like this:

"Saw Mrs Jones... She has ten children... Husband lost his arm in an accident... Did my best to find a job for Lily." He skipped on. His own name occurred less frequently. His interest slackened. Some of the entries conveyed nothing to him. For example: "Had a heated argument about socialism with B.M." Who was B.M.? He could not fill in the initials – some woman, he supposed, that she had met on one of her committees. "B.M. made a violent attack upon the upper classes... I walked back after the meeting with B.M. and tried to convince him. But he is so narrow-minded." So B.M. was a man – no doubt one of those "intellectuals", as they call themselves, who are so violent, as Angela said, and so narrow-minded. She had invited him to come and see her, apparently. "B.M. came to dinner. He shook hands with Minnie!" That note of exclamation gave another twist to his mental picture. B.M., it seemed, wasn't used to parlourmaids; he had shaken hands with Minnie. Presumably he was one of those tame working men who air their views in ladies' drawing rooms. Gilbert knew the type, and had no liking for this particular specimen, whoever B.M. might be. Here he was again. "Went with B.M. to the Tower of London... He said revolution is bound to come... He said we live in a fool's paradise." That was just the kind of thing B.M. would say – Gilbert could hear him. He could also see him quite distinctly – a stubby little man with a rough beard, red tie, dressed as they always did in tweeds, who had never done an honest day's work in his life. Surely Angela had the sense to see through him? He read on. "B.M. said some very disagreeable things about..." The name was carefully scratched out. "I told him I would not listen to any more abuse of..." Again the name was obliterated. Could it have been his own name? Was that why Angela covered the page so quickly when he came in? The thought added to his growing dislike of B.M. He had had the impertinence to discuss him in this very room. Why had Angela never told him? It was very unlike her to conceal anything; she had been the soul of candour. He turned the pages, picking out every reference to B.M. "B.M. told me the story of his childhood. His mother went out charring... When

I think of it, I can hardly bear to go on living in such luxury...
Three guineas for one hat!" If only she had discussed the matter
with him, instead of puzzling her poor little head about questions
that were much too difficult for her to understand! He had lent her
books. Karl Marx, 'The Coming Revolution'.* The initials B.M.,
B.M., B.M., recurred repeatedly. But why never the full name?
There was an informality, an intimacy in the use of initials that
was very unlike Angela. Had she called him B.M. to his face? He
read on. "B.M. came unexpectedly after dinner. Luckily, I was
alone." That was only a year ago. "Luckily" – why luckily? – "I
was alone." Where had he been that night? He checked the date
in his engagement book. It had been the night of the Mansion
House dinner. And B.M. and Angela had spent the evening alone!
He tried to recall that evening. Was she waiting up for him when
he came back? Had the room looked just as usual? Were there
glasses on the table? Were the chairs drawn close together? He
could remember nothing – nothing whatever, nothing except his
own speech at the Mansion House dinner. It became more and
more inexplicable to him – the whole situation... his wife receiving
an unknown man alone. Perhaps the next volume would explain.
Hastily he reached for the last of the diaries – the one she had
left unfinished when she died. There, on the very first page, was
that cursed fellow again. "Dined alone with B.M.... He became
very agitated. He said it was time we understood each other... I
tried to make him listen. But he would not. He threatened that if
I did not..." The rest of the page was scored over. She had written
"Egypt. Egypt. Egypt" over the whole page. He could not make
out a single word, but there could be only one interpretation:
the scoundrel had asked her to become his mistress. Alone in his
room! The blood rushed to Gilbert Clandon's face. He turned
the pages rapidly. What had been her answer? Initials had ceased.
It was simply "he" now. "He came again. I told him I could not
come to any decision... I implored him to leave me." He had forced
himself upon her in this very house. But why hadn't she told him?
How could she have hesitated for an instant? Then: "I wrote him

a letter." Then pages were left blank. Then there was this: "No answer to my letter." Then more blank pages, and then this: "He has done what he threatened." After that – what came after that? He turned page after page. All were blank. But there, on the very day before her death, was this entry: "Have I the courage to do it too?" That was the end.

Gilbert Clandon let the book slide to the floor. He could see her in front of him. She was standing on the kerb in Piccadilly. Her eyes stared; her fists were clenched. Here came the car...

He could not bear it. He must know the truth. He strode to the telephone.

"Miss Miller!" There was silence. Then he heard someone moving in the room.

"Sissy Miller speaking" – her voice at last answered him.

"Who," he thundered, "is B.M.?"

He could hear the cheap clock ticking on her mantelpiece, then a long-drawn sigh. Then at last she said:

"He was my brother."

He *was* her brother – her brother who had killed himself. "Is there," he heard Sissy Miller asking, "anything that I can explain?"

"Nothing!" he cried. "Nothing!"

He had received his legacy. She had told him the truth. She had stepped off the kerb to rejoin her lover. She had stepped off the kerb to escape from him.

Abbreviations

BP   *Books and Portraits* (1977)
DM   *The Death of the Moth* (1942)
HH   *A Haunted House and Other Stories* (1944)
MDP *Mrs Dalloway's Party* (1973)

Note on the Texts

Unless otherwise specified in the notes, the texts are taken from the first published edition of the stories.

Notes

p. 3, *Solid Objects*: First published in *The Athenaeum* (22nd October 1920) and reprinted in HH.

p. 6, *the Temple*: A group of buildings on Fleet Street, location of the Inner and Outer Temple, two of London's Inns of Court.

p. 10, *In the Orchard*: First published in *Criterion* (April 1923) and later in BP.

p. 10, *Ce pays... éclate le mieux*: "This country is truly one of the corners of the world where the laughter of girls breaks out most easily." The book Miranda is reading is *Ramuntcho* (1897), a novel of love and adventure by Pierre Loti (1850–1923). The quotation is from the beginning of Chapter 14.

p. 10, *Hymns Ancient and Modern*: A hymnal in common use within the Church of England.

p. 13, *Mrs Dalloway in Bond Street*: First published in *The Dial* (July 1923) and later collected in MDP, a sequence of seven stories that share some characters and situations with Woolf's novel *Mrs Dalloway* (1925). 'Mrs Dalloway in Bond Street' is an alternative version of the first pages of the published novel. The other stories in the sequence are 'Ancestors', 'The Introduction', 'Together and Apart', 'The Man Who Loved His Kind', 'A Summing-Up' and 'The New Dress'.

p. 13, *Justin Parry*: The father of Mrs Clarissa Dalloway.

p. 13, *CB*: Companion of (the Order of) the Bath.

p. 14, *Victoria's white mound*: The Victoria Memorial, a monument to Queen Victoria located at the end of The Mall.

p. 14, *The king and queen*: King George V and his consort Queen Mary.

p. 15, *the South African War*: The Second Boer War (1899–1902), fought between the British Empire and the independent Boer republics of the South African Republic and the Orange Free State (in present-day South Africa).

p. 15, *the park*: Green Park (officially "The Green Park").

p. 15, *Sir Dighton*: The British Army officer Sir Dighton Probyn (1833–1924).

p. 15, *And now can never mourn… slow stain*: Clarissa is recalling ll. 356–58 of *Adonais* (1821), a pastoral elegy written on the death of John Keats (1795–1821) by Percy Bysshe Shelley (1792–1822): "From the contagion of the world's slow stain / He is secure, and now can never mourn / A heart grown cold, a head grown grey in vain."

p. 15, *Have drunk their cup a round or two before*: The quotation is from *The Rubáiyát of Omar Khayyám* (XXI, l. 3), a translation by Edward FitzGerald (1809–83) of the work of the Persian astronomer and poet Omar Khayyam (1048–1131).

p. 16, *Sir Joshua perhaps, or Romney*: The English portrait painters Sir Joshua Reynolds (1723–92) and George Romney (1734–1802).

p. 16, *Soapy Sponge*: A reference to *Mr Sponge's Sporting Tour* (1853) by R.S. Surtees (1805–64). The book's eponymous hero is nicknamed by his friends "Soapy Sponge".

p. 16, *Cranford*: An 1853 novel by Elizabeth Gaskell (1810–65).

p. 16, *Was there ever… the cow in petticoats*: The first chapter of *Cranford* describes Miss Betsy Barker's beloved Alderney cow going to pasture "dressed in grey flannel".

p. 16, *Fear no more the heat o' the sun*: *Cymbeline*, Act IV, Sc. 2, l. 259.

p. 17, *Aeolian Hall*: A concert hall and small opera house.

p. 21, *Sargent*: The portrait painter John Singer Sargent (1856–1925), an American artist who spent a large part of his life abroad.

p. 21, *Thou thy worldly task hast done*: *Cymbeline*, Act IV, Sc. 2, l. 261.

p. 21, *a violent explosion in the street outside*: "The violent explosion which made Mrs Dalloway jump and Miss Pym go to the window and apologize came from a motor car which had drawn to the side of the pavement precisely opposite Mulberry's shop window" (*Mrs Dalloway*).

p. 22, *Ancestors*: Written in May 1925 and first published in MDP.

p. 24, *sweet Alice*: Sweet alyssum, a herbaceous plant.

p. 24, *shaved*: Amended from "stared", based on a holograph draft of the story.

p. 24, *'Ode to the West Wind'*: A poem by Percy Bysshe Shelley.

p. 26, *The Introduction*: Written after mid-March 1925 and first published in MDP.

p. 26, *Dean Swift*: The Anglo-Irish satirist Jonathan Swift (1667–1745).

p. 27, *melting*: Amended from "wilting", based on a holograph draft of the story.

p. 28, *it was partly... little chivalries*: Amended from "it was part of the dress, and all the little chivalries", based on the holograph draft.

p. 29, *carefulness*: Amended from "carelessness", based on the holograph draft.

p. 29, *ultimate*: Amended from "intimate", based on the holograph draft.

p. 32, *Together and Apart*: First published in MDP.

p. 32, *the Conqueror*: William the Conqueror (*c.*1027–87).

p. 33, *"On, Stanley, on"*: The last words pronounced by Marmion, before his death at the Battle of Flodden (1513), in Walter Scott's eponymous narrative poem of 1808.

p. 33, *and*: Amended from "but", based on a typescript of the story with holograph revisions.

p. 34, *Wordsworth's*: The English poet William Wordsworth (1770–1850).

p. 35, *repeat*: Amended from "respect", based on the typescript.

p. 38, *the Meistersinger*: *Die Meistersinger von Nürnberg* (*The Master-Singers of Nuremberg*), an opera by Richard Wagner (1813–83).

p. 39, *The Man Who Loved His Kind*: First published in HH and later reprinted in MDP, from where the text is taken.

p. 39, *Dean's Yard*: A large gated quadrangle in Westminster, part of the precincts of Westminster Abbey and adjoining on one side Westminster School.

p. 39, *Newcastle*: Eton College's most prestigious academic prize.

p. 43, *The Tempest*: A play by William Shakespeare.

p. 46, *A Summing-Up*: First published in HH and later reprinted in MDP, from where the text is taken.

p. 46, *Bradshaw*: The name of a railway timetable issued at regular intervals in Britain between 1839 and 1961 and named after the publisher George Bradshaw (1800–53).

p. 48, *the Isle of Thorney*: The small island on the Thames where Westminster Abbey and the Palace of Westminster were built in medieval times.

p. 49, *by a stone thrown at it*: A holograph draft of the story ends with the following additional paragraph: "It now appeared that during the conversation to which Sasha had scarcely listened Bertram had come to the conclusion that he liked Mr Wallace, but disliked his wife – who was 'very clever, no doubt'."

p. 50, *A Woman's College from Outside*: First published in *Atalanta's Garland* (1926), a collection of stories and poems by various authors commemorating the twenty-first anniversary of the foundation of the Edinburgh University Women's Union, and later reprinted in BP.

p. 50, *The feathery-white moon… meadows*: This initial sentence was reused by Woolf in *Jacob's Room* (Chapter 3).

p. 50, *Newnham*: A women's college of the University of Cambridge, founded in 1871.

p. 52, *Bamburgh Castle*: A castle on the coast of Northumberland (spelt "Bamborough" in the original). Woolf spent a month in that region in August 1914.

p. 54, *The New Dress*: First published in *The Forum* (May 1927) and later reprinted in HH.

p. 54, *Borrow or Scott*: The novelists George Borrow (1803–81) and Walter Scott (1771–1832).

p. 55, *guineas*: A guinea was worth twenty-one shillings, that is, one pound and one shilling.

p. 55, *the Empire*: The Second French Empire (1852–70).

p. 55, *We are all like flies trying to crawl over the edge of the saucer*: Probably an allusion to Chekhov's novella *The Duel* (Chapter 14): "And it seemed to her that all the evil memories in her head had taken shape and were walking beside her in the darkness, breathing heavily, while she, like a fly that had fallen into the inkpot, was crawling painfully along the pavement and smirching Laevsky's side and arm with blackness" (tr. Constance Garnett).

p. 56, *"Lies, lies, lies!"*: Another probable allusion to Chekhov's *The Duel* (Chapter 17): "He had not said one good word, not written one line that was not useless and vulgar; he had not done his fellows one ha'p'orth of service, but had eaten their bread, drunk their wine, seduced their wives, lived on their thoughts, and to justify his contemptible, parasitic life in their eyes and in his own, he had always tried to assume an air of being higher and better than they. Lies, lies, lies…" (tr. Constance Garnett).

p. 56, *scrolloping*: A word invented by Woolf to denote something that is convoluted or overly florid (also used by Woolf in *Orlando* and *The Waves*).

p. 57, *We're all weevils in a captain's biscuit*: Possibly an allusion to *Treasure Island* by Robert Louis Stevenson (1850–94): "If you had the pluck of a weevil in a biscuit you would catch them still" (Chapter 5). A "captain's biscuit" is a hard variety of fancy biscuit.

p. 57, *Boadicea*: Boadicea (Boudicca) was the queen of the ancient British Iceni tribe who led a failed uprising against the occupying Roman forces in 60–61 AD.

p. 59, *a threepenny bit*: A coin worth three old pence.

p. 59, *cormorants*: Cormorants are proverbial for their voracity.

p. 60, *Sir Henry Lawrence*: Sir Henry Montgomery Lawrence (1806–57), a military officer and administrator in British India.

p. 60, *the Law Courts*: An informal name for the Royal Courts of Justice, located on the Strand in central London.

p. 63, *"Slater's Pins Have No Points"*: First published in *The Forum* (January 1928) and later reprinted, with some changes, under the title 'Moments of Being: "Slater's Pins Have No Points"' in HH.

p. 66, *the Tubes*: A colloquial name (usually "the Tube") for the underground railway network in London.

p. 66, *Browning*: The English poet Robert Browning (1812–89).

p. 66, *the Serpentine*: A recreational lake in Hyde Park.

p. 68, *Brompton Road*: A London street running from Knightsbridge to the top of the Fulham Road, in what was (and still is) an affluent residential area of the city.

p. 70, *Three Pictures*: Written in June 1929 and first published in DM.

p. 74, *The Lady in the Looking Glass: A Reflection*: First published in *Harper's Magazine* (December 1929) and reprinted in HH.

p. 80, *The Shooting Party*: First published in *Harper's Bazaar* (March 1938) and reprinted, with some changes, in HH.

p. 85, *Old Miss Rashleigh filled her glass*: This sentence, which does not appear in the first edition (*Harper's Bazaar*), has been restored from the text published in HH.

p. 87, *tawse*: A thong with a slit end used as a whip.

p. 89, *The Duchess and the Jeweller*: First published in *Harper's Bazaar* (April 1938) and reprinted in HH.

p. 95, *Agincourt*: The site of a famous English victory against France (1415).

p. 96, *Lappin and Lapinova*: First published in *Harper's Bazaar* (April 1939) and reprinted in HH.

p. 96, *the Albert Memorial… the Prince Consort*: References to Prince Albert (1819–61), the husband of Queen Victoria (1819–1901), to commemorate whom an ornate pavilion, designed in the Gothic Revival style by Sir George Gilbert Scott (1811–78) and completed in 1872, was erected in Kensington Gardens. A statue of the prince was placed inside in 1876.

p. 99, *an apple-pie bed*: A bed which has been made with one of the sheets folded back on itself, so as to make it impossible for a person to get into it.

p. 105, *The Searchlight*: First published in HH.

p. 110, *The Legacy*: First published in HH.

p. 113, *Florian's*: Caffè Florian, in Piazza San Marco.

p. 116, *'The Coming Revolution'*: 'The Coming Revolution' (1913) is a political article by the Irish nationalist Patrick Pearse (1879–1916).

Extra Material

on

Virginia Woolf's

*The New Dress
and Other Stories*

Virginia Woolf's Life

Virginia Woolf was born Adeline Virginia Stephen on 25th *Birth and* January 1882 at her family's residence at 22 Hyde Park Gate, *Background* London. Her father was the renowned writer, critic and mountaineer Leslie Stephen, who was the first editor of the *Dictionary of National Biography*, and her mother was Julia Prinsep Stephen, famous for her beauty and philanthropy, whose family included the photographer Julia Margaret Cameron and the painter Valentine Cameron Prinsep. Both parents had children from previous marriages: Leslie Stephen's union with Harriet Marian Thackeray, daughter of the novelist, which had ended with the latter's death in 1875, had produced a daughter, Laura, in 1870, and Julia Stephen had given birth to two sons, George (born in 1868) and Gerald (born in 1870), and a daughter, Stella (born in 1869), before the death of her first husband Herbert Duckworth in 1870. In addition to Virginia, the Stephens had three children together: Vanessa (born in 1879), Thoby (born in 1880) and Adrian (born in 1883).

Virginia's childhood was spent largely at the elegant but *Childhood* somewhat cramped family home in Kensington and, during the summer, at Talland House, her father's country residence near St Ives in Cornwall. The summer house was always in something of a state of disrepair, but the location was idyllic and had a lasting impression on Virginia's life and subsequent work. In both homes the Stephen children were exposed to the distinguished social gatherings organized by their parents, and although these occasions no doubt provided much stimulation, the strict adherence to convention also had a stifling effect, especially on the girls.

The relationships between the children were complex: although Virginia, Vanessa, Thoby and Adrian tended to band together against their older half-siblings – in the case of the intellectually challenged Laura it was sometimes a case of cruel rejection – and would often engage in creative activities together, there were rivalries and jealousies between the four as well, especially between Virginia and Vanessa. But despite their differences, the two sisters would share a close bond throughout their adult lives and collaborate artistically, with Vanessa becoming an established painter.

Education Apart from Greek classes at King's College and lessons with private tutors when she was in her teens, Virginia was exclusively educated at home, receiving instruction from her father – who had been a Cambridge don – every morning. In addition to this high-calibre personal tuition, he gave his daughter full access to the books in his library, and she read voraciously – from the classics of English and European literature to voluminous histories and biographies. Her father's taste had a considerable influence on her and she developed a similar penchant for biographical writing very early on, penning personal journals and family histories, and collaborating with her siblings on a mock newspaper about the Stephen household entitled *Hyde Park Gate News*, as well as a serialized romance about their neighbours, the Dilkes. These early literary endeavours were not only a result of her desire to emulate her father and satisfy her own creative urges, but also an attempt to gain the attention of her mother, whose commendations, it appears, she especially craved.

Death of The happiness and security enjoyed by Virginia were rocked
Mother and First in May 1895 by the unexpected death of her mother from what
Breakdown had started as influenza but developed into a rheumatic fever. Naturally, this event was immensely painful for the thirteen-year-old and would plunge her into a state of depression and temporarily quell her creative output. She experienced what is commonly referred to as her first breakdown, from which it seems she took around a year to recover, treated mainly by Dr Seton, the family doctor; but as there is not much documentary evidence surviving about this episode, the exact nature of her ailment remains unclear. Virginia's own reminiscences do not explicitly describe any form of mental illness, but she does

ascribe some favourable significance to the day her mother died and its effects, claiming they helped shape and heighten her artistic perceptions, "as if a burning glass has been laid over what was shaded and dormant".

Julia's place as matriarch in the disconsolate household was *Death of Stella* taken by her daughter Stella, who herself tragically died only two years later – at the young age of twenty-eight and having recently married – of complications following an operation. The death of her half-sister shattered Virginia and left her reeling at a delicate stage in her own development, as she later wrote: "The blow, the *second* blow of death, struck on me: tremulous, creased, sitting with my wings still stuck together in the broken chrysalis."

These deaths were not the only traumas that marred her youth *Sexual Abuse* and contributed to her mental distress: she was subjected to humiliation and sexual molestation by her half-brother Gerald, twelve years her senior, the earliest recorded incident of which occurred when she was only six and he explored her genitalia. This terrifying event, of which she naturally did not dare to speak at the time, had a devastating impact on her self-esteem, her health and her view of sexuality and men. After the deaths of her mother and Stella, it appears that Gerald intensified his attentions as well as belittling her in public. The extent and nature of his improprieties are unclear, and Virginia's own assertions are contradictory: at one point she claimed that her half-brother had been her first lover, whereas later she suggested that it had not gone as far as that physically – but in any case his behaviour was mentally scarring for the young woman.

To make matters worse, a second wave of deaths in the *Death of Father* family began in 1904, when her father died on 22nd February after a period of illness. Virginia had been feeling conflicting emotions about him, resenting him as an authority figure and even describing him as a tyrant, but she had been dreading his impending death not only because of the disarray she felt it would bring into the family, but also because her tender feelings towards him were resurfacing.

Two and half months after her father's death she experienced *Second Breakdown* her second breakdown. As with the first, the lack of recorded information means it is difficult to form a precise impression of the exact sequence and nature of events, but it seems that it

took her three months to recover and that in the summer she
may have made a suicide attempt by jumping out of a window.

Mental Health   Further breakdowns would occur, usually involving delirium,
violent mood swings, suicidal impulses and a refusal to eat, and
throughout her life it is clear that Virginia Woolf was afflicted
by acute recurring mental illness, but an accurate diagnosis
is still subject to dispute. In her time she was often labelled
neurasthenic, a vague and dated term, but to use modern-day
medical language she was probably suffering from bipolar
disorder, commonly referred to as manic depression.

One consequence of the relatively unsophisticated
understanding of mental illness that existed at the time was
that the methods used by the doctors overseeing her were
authoritarian and rudimentary, often limited to forcing her to
eat and rest and administering sedatives. In fact, it is at times
unclear whether certain symptoms, such as hallucinations, were
the result of her illness or the treatment. Virginia took a very
dim view of her doctors, especially Dr George Savage, who was
responsible for her care during her 1904 breakdown and for some
years to follow. He had previously tended to her cousin, the poet
James Kenneth Stephen, a tragic figure who also suffered from
mental illness, and he tended to send his patients, including
Virginia, to oppressive nursing homes and sanatoriums.

Bloomsbury   After the death of Leslie Stephen, Vanessa arranged for
Virginia, Thoby, Adrian and herself to move into a new residence:
46 Gordon Square in Bloomsbury. In this location they finally
felt liberated from the constraints of the paternal home, and
associated with similarly cerebral friends, an informal network
which would gradually come to be referred to as the Bloomsbury
Group. It would include figures such as E.M. Forster, John
Maynard Keynes, Lytton Strachey, the artists Roger Fry and
Duncan Grant, and Virginia and Vanessa's future husbands,
Leonard Woolf and the art critic Clive Bell respectively. The group
distinguished itself not only by the high artistic and intellectual
calibre of its members, but also by its progressive ideals, casting
aside Victorian orthodoxy in favour of sexual and social freedom,
granting women the role of equals, accepting homosexuals and
tolerating extramarital relationships.

Modernism   While the Bloomsbury Group was a stepping stone to social
and intellectual liberation, artistically Virginia Woolf would

become part of the wider movement known as Modernism. As the world was moving away from the certainties and conventions of the nineteenth century to one in which scientific advance and social and political unrest challenged previously held perceptions, the arts had to find new modes of expression to reflect these shifts. Ushered in by the works of Joseph Conrad and Henry James, the literary Modernists of the 1910s and 1920s such as T.S. Eliot, Wyndham Lewis, Marcel Proust, James Joyce and Ezra Pound all contributed in their own way to a more experimental approach to writing. Virginia Woolf, who in 1924 remarked that "on or about December 1910, human character changed", would gradually find her voice within this new artistic context and rapidly become one of Modernism's figureheads.

The relocation to Bloomsbury did not bring an end to the *Death of Thoby* family's misfortunes, and, just as the death of Virginia's mother was closely followed by Stella's, her father's passing soon ushered in another family tragedy. In September and October 1906, Virginia, Vanessa, Thoby and Adrian travelled through Greece with their friend Violet Dickinson (with whom Virginia had formed a romantic relationship); Vanessa and Thoby fell ill and were bedridden on their return to England. While Vanessa's state improved, her brother was diagnosed with typhoid fever and died. Virginia had become very close to Thoby who, although reserved and mysterious, had embodied a more tender form of masculinity. This painful bereavement was accompanied by the symbolic loss of Vanessa, whose engagement to Clive Bell shortly afterwards represented to Virginia the end of their relationship as sisters. However, this time her grief apparently did not lead to depression or a nervous breakdown.

Ever since the emancipatory move to Bloomsbury, Virginia, *Early Writing* energized by the intellectual encounters she was having, was writing even more profusely. She was now convinced that she would make a career out of it, declaring in September 1904, "I know I can write, and one of these days I mean to produce a good book." On top of her personal reminiscences and essays – which she started publishing first in an Anglican journal called the *Guardian* and later in the *Times Literary Supplement* – she completed a first mature attempt at fiction, a story entitled 'Phyllis and Rosamond', in 1906.

In addition to writing, from 1905 to 1907 she also gave evening lessons at Morley College in south London, an establishment for adult education aimed at workers. Although she was initially only to lecture on English grammar, she insisted on teaching history, and took her task very seriously, emerging from the experience with a stronger sense of confidence and purpose.

In 1908 she began experimenting on a full-length novel entitled *Melymbrosia*. The gestation of this first novel would prove to be long and arduous, however, causing her much anxiety in the process. Another source of unease was her struggle to understand her own sexual identity: although she had been exploring her homosexual feelings, she found herself attracted to men, notably Clive Bell, a situation which provoked her sister's jealousy. Added to this was her fear that she would remain single, childless and increasingly dependent on Vanessa.

In the summer of 1910, when Virginia showed signs of another mental collapse, Vanessa consulted Dr Savage, who recommended a stay at a sanatorium in Twickenham run by the pious Jean Thomas. Virginia spent six weeks there, complaining of her treatment, accusing her sister of conspiracy and threatening to jump out of the window.

Marriage to Leonard Woolf   In August 1912, Virginia married Leonard Woolf, a friend of Thoby's from his Cambridge days and the son of a Jewish barrister, whom she had first met in 1904, before he had left Britain to become a colonial administrator in Ceylon. He had resigned from that post a few months before the wedding, and from then on would focus his energies on his political writing. Despite their difference in social background and Virginia's occasional anti-Semitism and initial hesitation about accepting his proposal, the two developed a deep bond, which manifested itself emotionally and professionally, if not always sexually. Leonard generally read and offered advice on everything his wife wrote and supported her through her bouts of mental illness, which he documented at considerable length.

Further Breakdowns   The year 1913 would be a testing one for the couple: all the while working hard on her novel – which she had by now completely reinvented under the title *The Voyage Out* and which had been accepted for publication by Gerald Duckworth's fledgling imprint – Virginia, whose mental health had been fragile, was plagued by terrible feelings of inadequacy as a writer, wife and sister, which resulted in a further breakdown and suicide attempt by overdose of medication in September. During this period Leonard consulted various neurologists and it was decided that Virginia should convalesce, under medical supervision, in the Sussex countryside. By spring 1914 she had recovered and later that year the couple moved to Richmond, Surrey.

Early in the following year Virginia suffered another violent breakdown, which required a further period of constant supervision, as it was feared that in her delirium she would be a danger to herself again. The impending publication of *The Voyage Out* was an important contributing factor to her distress, as she was terrified by the reception it would get, particularly after having read Leonard's recently published novel *The Wise Virgins*, which contained a character unflatteringly based on her. By the end of the year she was on the path to recovery again; her debut novel, meanwhile, had been published in March and was attracting positive reviews, with some already seeing in her the spark of genius and innovation. Her career as a novelist was off to a promising start.

Meanwhile, the great powers of Europe had been plunged *First World War* into a major conflict. Although Virginia Woolf did not have any first-hand experience of the Great War, the cataclysmic event would have a significant effect on her life and writings. It reinforced her staunch personal belief in pacifism – a stance that she would never give up – and would play an important role in her fiction: as a defining event not described directly but happening "offstage", and in the form of characters dying or being traumatized by their involvement in it. More generally, the conflict and the disillusionment, and loss of innocence it entailed, were crucial in shaping the Modernist aesthetic and approach, favouring a shift towards fragmented texts and more uncertain, less authoritative narrative voices – elements which would feature prominently in Virginia Woolf's mature works.

In 1917 the Woolfs bought a printing machine and installed *Hogarth Press* it in their home in Richmond, and established Hogarth Press, named after their home, Hogarth House. This venture had modest ambitions at first: it was an experiment in printing their own works; but soon it became a major publishing house, producing books not only by members of the Bloomsbury Group such as E.M. Forster, Clive Bell, Roger Fry and John Maynard Keynes, but also by the likes of T.S. Eliot, Robert Graves, Edith Sitwell and a multitude of international, mainly Russian, authors (Maxim Gorky, Ivan Bunin, Leonid Andreyev). Owning Hogarth Press would play a crucial part in the evolution of her own work: she now had full control of the creative development of her books, down to typesetting and production, and they would often contain woodcuts by her sister Vanessa. After Virginia Woolf's death, the press would also publish the major psychoanalytical works of its day.

Charleston and Monk's House

Having often holidayed in the Sussex countryside, both Vanessa and Virginia acquired homes there. In 1916 Vanessa moved to a farmhouse called Charleston with her children but without Clive Bell – they had both been involved with other lovers for some time, despite remaining on good terms; she conducted long-term affairs first with Roger Fry and then with Duncan Grant, who joined her in Charleston. The house became a home from home for various bohemians, artists and writers. Three years later the Woolfs bought the nearby Monk's House in the village of Rodmell, where they would spend summers.

Second Novel

In the early days of Hogarth Press Virginia worked on her second novel, entitled *Night and Day*, and it was published in 1919. To the surprise and dismay of some, this book was, in terms of stylistic innovation, a step backwards, and it is still considered her most traditional and Victorian work. She would later claim that this temporary shift towards narrative conventionalism was due to the fact that in her fragile state of mind at the time she did not dare attempt anything too bold and potentially dangerous.

But this did not mean Virginia was steering off course in her revolutionary mission: indeed she began explicitly to theorize her conception of the future of prose fiction in essays such as the 1919 'Modern Novels', in which she criticized the living practitioners of what she called "materialist" fiction, H.G. Wells, John Galsworthy and Arnold Bennett (describing the last as "catching life just an inch or two on the wrong side"), and praised the "spiritualists", in particular James Joyce, whose *A Portrait of the Artist as a Young Man* (published in 1916) and *Ulysses* (then being serialized) she regarded as epitomizing the new approach to literature she was seeking to advocate: "he disregards with complete courage whatever seems to him adventitious, though it be probability or coherence or any other of the handrails to which we cling for support when we set our imaginations free." This new style was one that avoided the traps of realist prose, such as chronology, plot, superficial realism and objectivity, and instead investigated the unsaid and the unsayable, while exploring poetically the workings of consciousness. She illustrated these theories in various short pieces that were published in the 1921 collection *Monday or Tuesday*, a work that unfortunately attracted limited critical attention at the time – something that upset the author and momentarily halted the progress of her third novel.

That novel, entitled *Jacob's Room*, eventually appeared in 1922, the year that is often considered the high-water mark of literary Modernism, witnessing as it did the publication of Joyce's *Ulysses* and T.S. Eliot's *The Waste Land*. It was not only bold stylistically, in contrast to *Night and Day*, but also in terms of the personal subject matter it addressed: in this case Virginia's feelings of loss relating to the death of her brother Thoby. Unfortunately, although its innovative qualities were beyond dispute and it is now considered a cornerstone of Modernist writing, readers and critics failed to warm to it, as its fragmentary minimalism and stripping-away of plot made for an alienating read. *[Third Novel]*

That same year Virginia met Vita Sackville-West, the extravagant aristocratic writer, who embodied for her the strong, sensual, confident side of femininity, which Virginia felt herself to be lacking, and in 1925 they began a sexual relationship. Vita would be the inspiration for Woolf's semi-biographical fantasy *Orlando* (1928).

Virginia had became tired of life in suburban Richmond and yearned to return to central London and its dynamic social life. Although Leonard originally opposed the idea as he felt concerned for his wife's mental health, the couple moved back to Bloomsbury in March 1924, renting a property on Tavistock Square. The offices of Hogarth Press were moved into the basement of the building. *[Move Back to Bloomsbury]*

It was back in London that Virginia would publish the novels for which she is now most acclaimed. *Mrs Dalloway*, *[Major Novels]* although begun when she was still living in Richmond and recasting a character, Clarissa Dalloway, from *The Voyage Out*, is clearly infused with London social life, centring as it does on the preparations for an upper-middle-class dinner party. While in some ways the novel marked a return to a more linear form of storytelling and contains a prominent protagonist – unlike *Jacob's Room*, in which the titular character is largely absent – it did not abandon avant-garde techniques in the least: in fact it was revolutionary in the way it interwove the consciousnesses of two separate characters. Upon publication in 1925, *Mrs Dalloway* received overwhelmingly positive reviews.

Virginia Woolf built on the breakthrough success of *Mrs Dalloway* with another display of stylistic innovation combined with emotional resonance and deft characterization: *To the Lighthouse*, published in 1927. Using a rigid tripartite structure as a framework for an elegiac stream-of-consciousness exploration of time, the novel confirmed that its author was at the height of her fiction-writing powers.

Political Activism   But it is a testament to the scope of Virginia Woolf's ambitions and talents that she was not content with triumph in the sphere of fiction. In fact, her concerns as a novelist overlapped with her concerns as a historian, critic and political activist, and one of the main focuses of all of these pursuits was the issue of women and their role in the world. Her personal history had made her acutely aware of the subjugation of women from an early age and she had become conscious of the feminist cause when at the age of twenty she received Greek lessons from Janet Case, who was an advocate for women's rights. In 1910 she started volunteering for the women's suffrage movement and many of her reviews and historical writings were aimed at investigating the lives of women. Her activism would take on a new dimension in 1929, when she published *A Room of One's Own*, based on talks she had given at Cambridge. In this seminal essay she argued that women had been marginalized, largely omitted from historical record and that their potential in the public sphere had never been allowed to flourish due to economic and social constraints – that in order to do so a woman "must have money and a room of her own". This was followed in 1931 by *Professions for Women*, which looked more specifically into the inequality of educational and professional opportunities for women throughout history. She would never cease to speak out against and write about female oppression for the rest of her life.

It was also thanks to the publication of *A Room of One's Own* that in 1930 Virginia met Dame Ethel Smyth, the composer and leading figure of the British suffragette movement. The two, although very different in character, saw themselves as kindred spirits and formed a close, platonic relationship that was at times tempestuous.

The year 1931 saw the publication of *The Waves*. Considered *Later Novels* by some to be Virginia Woolf's boldest novel stylistically and the pinnacle of her novelistic project in its blurring and interweaving of six different characters and their consciousnesses, it has, however, never achieved the popularity of *Mrs Dalloway* or *To the Lighthouse*. Woolf's next novel further demonstrated her continued quest for new forms of experimentation. *The Years* (1937) had originated in a project entitled *The Pargiters*, which was to integrate political and historical essays into a fictional chronicle spanning fifty years in the life of one family and highlighting issues of violence and discrimination towards women. The work proved too cumbersome and difficult to complete, however, and so Woolf decided to do away with the essays, resulting in a novel that became a resounding commercial success.

In 1937 the worsening international situation had a direct *The Threat of War* impact on Virginia's family, when Vanessa's son Julian was killed in the Spanish Civil War. Virginia interrupted her creative activities to support her devastated sister, but the event inspired her to write the treatise *Three Guineas*, published in 1938, which linked together feminism and pacifism and characterized war as the foremost excess of masculine authority. This stance was not without controversy at the time, when Britain, on the brink of conflict, was being whipped up into a patriotic fervour.

This ominous pre-war atmosphere and various deaths among *Final Years* her circle – her close friend Roger Fry's in 1934 and Lady Ottoline Morrell's in 1938, in addition to Julian's mentioned above – cast the pall of death over Virginia's final years. She continued to write, juggling various projects such as her biography of Fry, her own memoirs and what would be her final novel, *Between the Acts* (published posthumously in 1941). Although this activity constituted her way of overcoming her demons and the horrors of her times, by the time London was being bombed in 1940 and 1941 she felt her "writing 'I'" slipping away from her and she was filled with doubt as to the purpose and efficacy of her art.

Suicide The Blitz forced the Woolfs to seek refuge in Monk's House, their cottage in Sussex. Fearing an imminent invasion, they prepared contingency plans to avoid being captured by the Germans (an especially terrifying prospect given that Leonard was Jewish), including a possible joint suicide. But the depression and isolation she felt got the better of her, and on 28th March 1941 she walked out of the house and, having weighed down her pockets with stones, drowned herself in the River Ouse. She was fifty-nine. She left behind the following suicide note to her husband:

> Dearest, I feel certain that I am going mad again. I feel we can't go through another of those terrible times. And I shan't recover this time. I begin to hear voices, and I can't concentrate. So I am doing what seems the best thing to do. You have given me the greatest possible happiness. You have been in every way all that anyone could be. I don't think two people could have been happier 'til this terrible disease came. I can't fight any longer. I know that I am spoiling your life, that without me you could work. And you will I know. You see I can't even write this properly. I can't read. What I want to say is I owe all the happiness of my life to you. You have been entirely patient with me and incredibly good. I want to say that – everybody knows it. If anybody could have saved me it would have been you. Everything has gone from me but the certainty of your goodness. I can't go on spoiling your life any longer. I don't think two people could have been happier than we have been. V.

Her body was found three weeks later, and after her cremation Leonard buried her ashes in the garden of Monk's House.

Virginia Woolf's output was prolific: apart from her nine novels, she left behind scores of short stories, hundreds of essays, thousands of letters and a diary that runs to thirty volumes – as well as two full-length biographies and even a play.

The Voyage Out, Woolf's first novel, was published on 26th *The Voyage Out* March 1915 by Gerald Duckworth & Co. after a long gestation period during which its author suffered much psychological torment. Work on the book began in 1908 under the working title *Melymbrosia*, but the author undertook radical changes to the plot and characters in 1912, while also toning down or removing most of the overtly political passages.

The story focuses on Rachel Vinrace, a young lady who embarks on a voyage with her aunt, uncle and father on a ship owned by the latter, the *Eufrosyne*, which first travels to Lisbon and then to the South American island of Santa Marina. They are joined on board by Clarissa and Richard Dalloway and the scholar William Pepper, and their conversations during the journey and what they reveal about their characters comprise the bulk of the first part of the novel. The second part takes place on Santa Marina, where the passengers have disembarked, both in the villa occupied by Rachel, her aunt and uncle and William Pepper, and the nearby hotel frequented by British tourists. The conversations and social interactions between the various characters unfold, while Rachel falls in love with the young novelist Terence Hewet. The two declare their feelings for each other while on an expedition to a native village and become engaged, but the romance is short-lived, as Rachel dies of illness upon her return.

Unsurprisingly for a first novel, *The Voyage Out* displays neither the skilfulness nor the ambition of Virginia Woolf's later fiction, but it contains many of the themes and images that would inform her future writing and found on publication enough positive critical acclaim to encourage the young author to continue to hone her craft.

Woolf's follow-up novel, *Night and Day*, was published on 20th *Night and Day* October 1919, again by Duckworth. She had begun writing it in early 1915 under the working title *The Third Generation*, and continued work on it in the aftermath of the serious breakdown she experienced that year. The novel is set in the fashionable circles of London and centres on Katharine Hilbery, who is helping her mother write the biography of her late grandfather, a famous poet. She becomes engaged to William Rodney, an alliance which is quickly shown to be a mismatch, since he is much more conservative than his freethinking fiancée. The latter begins to frequent the lower-middle-class solicitor Ralph Denham and the suffragette Mary Datchet. While Mary is in love with Ralph, he is in fact drawn to Katharine, but decides to pursue Mary anyway, and is on the verge of proposing to her when he sees Katharine walking down the street and goes back on his decision. Katharine is also affected by the attentions of Ralph and calls off her engagement to William, only to change her mind again when she sees how much she has upset him. The sentimental hesitations between the four continue for much of the novel, until William falls in love and becomes engaged to Katharine's cousin Cassandra, leaving Katharine free to betroth herself to Ralph. But as Ralph is from a lower social stratum than Katharine, her father is scandalized by this development and refuses to allow the union, until his far more indulgent wife convinces him to change his mind. The novel ends on a note of romantic triumph.

Although well-constructed and subtly balancing elements of farce and romance, *Night and Day* has bewildered readers of Woolf's fiction to this day, due to its conventionality. The notable critic Katherine Mansfield, who was also a friend of the author's, said of the novel: "It is impossible to refrain from comparing *Night and Day* with the novels of Miss Austen. There are moments, indeed, when one is almost tempted to cry it Miss Austen up-to-date." From the Modernist pioneer Mansfield, this was a stinging rebuke. But although it is something of an oddity in the Woolf canon, *Night and Day* does contain many highly poetic and symbolic descriptions and addresses themes that would remain crucial in her work, such as the suffrage movement and the tensions between love and marriage.

Jacob's Room   *Jacob's Room*, the first of Woolf's novels to be published by the Hogarth Press, on 26th October 1922, was a radical departure from its predecessors. With this book she set her fiction free from the shackles of linear plot and character, while addressing a deeply personal topic, the death of her brother Thoby from illness.

Although the novel is presented chronologically, there is no coherent story as such, rather a series of sketches and impressions chronicling the life of Jacob Flanders (a fictionalized Thoby), relating to his childhood in Cornwall, his schooldays, his time at Trinity College, Cambridge, his existence in London while studying for the Bar, his travels to Paris and Greece and his deployment to France as a young soldier, where he loses his life. The short fragments (some only a sentence long) that make up the text are written from the point of view of people (mostly women) who had known Jacob in his life, and many of them do not depict him directly. The book ends with a description of the contents of Jacob's room, as his mother and Richard Bonamy, a Cambridge friend, are sorting through his belongings.

While the public reception for *Jacob's Room* was relatively lukewarm and it is one of her lesser-read novels today, its avant-garde techniques (such as the systematic use of stream-of-consciousness narration and fragmented timelines) combined with its reflections on the nature of loss and the inherent impossibility of biography have ensured that it is regarded as Woolf's first truly experimental novel and one of the key texts in the Modernist canon.

On 14th May 1925, Woolf published one of her best-known *Mrs Dalloway* books, *Mrs Dalloway*, with Hogarth Press. She had written a short story, 'Mrs Dalloway in Bond Street', featuring Clarissa Dalloway, a character from her first novel, *The Voyage Out*, but then decided to work it into a full novel, initially entitled *The Hours*.

Mrs Dalloway is formed of two independent main narratives, which unfold over a single day in London: one details the activities of Clarissa Dalloway, the middle-aged wife of a Member of Parliament – as well as the pursuits of her family members and acquaintances – as she prepares to host an important party in the evening, while the other tells of the events leading to the suicide of Septimus Warren Smith, a severely shell-shocked war veteran. The two strands come together at the end of the novel when the specialist who had attended to Septimus earlier in the day attends the party at Mrs Dalloway's and tells of his story. Although the events portrayed are strictly confined to a single day, they give rise to flashbacks to earlier incidents in the characters' lives. Mrs Dalloway's morning begins with her buying flowers and reminiscing, when she meets an old friend, Hugh Whitbread; it continues with her receiving a visit from Peter Walsh, one of her old flames, her husband coming back from lunch with roses, and her conflict, unspoken but simmering below the surface, with her daughter's governess. It ends with her triumphant party, which is attended not only by the Prime Minister and the crème de la crème of London society, but also unexpectedly by a very old friend of hers, Sally Seton. Septimus Smith's day contrasts markedly with Mrs Dalloway's: it begins with him killing time in Regent's Park with his Italian wife Rezia, while waiting for a midday appointment with the celebrated psychiatrist Sir William Bradshaw, and we learn of his inner turmoil, largely brought on by the war and the horror of losing a close friend in the conflict. The doctor recommends a mental home for Septimus, but his wife is resistant to the idea and the couple go back to their lodgings. After a rest Septimus wakes up in good cheer, but his demons soon come back when his GP Dr Holmes appears, prompting Septimus to jump out of a window to his death. Upon learning of this tragic story at her party, Mrs Dalloway momentarily retreats to a private room to reflect on this event.

An innovative novel in which an ostensibly limited time frame and subject allow for an elaborate reflection on marriage, failed dreams and madness, as well as achieving what was, by Woolf's standards, a broad depiction of London life, *Mrs Dalloway* was the first work of fiction by Virginia Woolf which truly managed to strike a chord with critics and the public alike, and remains a Modernist classic to this day. It provides a compelling portrayal of the preoccupations of those of her milieu, while the subplot offers insight into her own personal experience of mental illness and the doctors who attempted to treat it. Stylistically speaking, it was arguably with this novel that Woolf perfected the stream-of-consciousness technique with which she has since become associated.

To the Lighthouse   *To the Lighthouse*, seen by many as Virginia Woolf's master-piece, was published by Hogarth Press on 5th May 1927. It was the most autobiographical book she had written so far, very much influenced by her childhood stays in the Stephen country house in Cornwall, and she was satisfied by the result, calling it "easily the best of my books".

Centring as it does mostly on dialogue, memories and descriptions and shifting between the various characters' consciousnesses, there is little action or plot to describe in *To the Lighthouse*. The novel is structured in three parts and set in the holiday home on the Isle of Skye belonging to the Ramsays, a family closely modelled on the Stephens.

The first part, 'The Window', begins with Mrs Ramsay telling her young son James that he will be able to visit the nearby lighthouse the next day, an expectation which is quashed by the rational philosopher Mr Ramsay, who claims the weather will be too foul. This event causes some resentment on the part of the mother and son towards the father, a motif that resonates throughout the novel. The reader is gradually introduced to the various guests at the house, such as the glum young researcher and admirer of Mr Ramsay, Charles Tansley, the budding painter Lily Briscoe, the opium-eating poet Augustus Carmichael, the botanist and widower William Bankes and Paul Rayley and Minta Doyle, a young man and woman whose romance is kindled during their stay at the Ramsays'. During the course of the day the reader is shown not only the interactions of the characters, but also their inner thoughts, especially those of Mrs Ramsay, as she speculates on the prospects of her young guests, pairs some of them off romantically in her mind and reflects on her family and relationship with her husband. Mrs Ramsay goes off on an errand with Charles Tansley, Paul proposes to Minta during a walk along the shore, Lily Briscoe embarks on a portrait of Mrs Ramsay, although she doubts her own abilities, before the evening ends with a dinner party meticulously organized Mrs Ramsay – which is a success, despite the brief annoyances occasioned by Paul and Minta's late arrival, due to her having lost her grandmother's brooch on the beach, and Mr Ramsay's brusque reaction to Augustus Carmichael's request for a second serving of soup. The chapter ends with the Ramsays quietly conversing in the parlour.

The brief second part, 'Time Passes', begins on the same evening, as lights are extinguished and members of the household go to bed. Then when night falls the narrative accelerates through the following years, during which, the reader learns, Mrs Ramsay passes away, her daughter Prue dies from complications related to childbirth, her son Andrew is killed in the trenches and Carmichael achieves great success as a poet. The house is left empty and falls into disrepair, and the section ends with a description of the housekeeper and her helpers getting the house ready for the return of the family and their guests ten years later.

When the third part, 'The Lighthouse', begins, some of the characters from the opening section have returned to the house. The narrative again shifts between the characters' thoughts, Lily Briscoe's being this time the most prominent, revealing to the reader her ongoing anxieties about painting, the difficulties Paul and Minta have encountered in their marriage and the void left by the loss of Mrs Ramsay. Mr Ramsay insists on finally making the trip to the lighthouse that had never materialized ten years earlier, and his youngest son and daughter, James and Cam, accompany him, even though they have both lost their enthusiasm for the project. But when they do arrive at their destination, they forget some of the resentment they have built up towards their father and feel a fond connection with him. The novel ends with Lily finally finishing her painting of Mrs Ramsay.

Remarkable for its moving, personal, elegiac tone, *To the Lighthouse* was another breakthrough in terms of Virginia Woolf's artistic development. Displaying little concern for straightforward storytelling, it is radical in its description of the transience of human life and achievement and stylistic mimicry of the complexity of perception. It arguably defies the category of "novel"; Leonard Woolf provided an apt label for it: "a psychological poem".

Orlando   Although considered by many, including its author, a "fantastical biography", *Orlando*, published in 1928 by Hogarth Press, is more often than not categorized as a novel, albeit one inspired by the life of the flamboyant writer Vita Sackville-West, Virginia's friend and sometime lover.

The story begins in England in 1586 and the reader is introduced to beautiful, poetry-writing young nobleman Orlando, who becomes a court favourite of Queen Elizabeth's. He attracts various aristocratic ladies but refuses any marital alliance, briefly cavorting with lower-class women before falling in love with the Russian Princess Sasha, whose subsequent unexpected return to her own country leaves him heartbroken. He retreats to his castle to work on his verse epic *The Oak Tree*, seeking the literary advice of the poet Nick Greene, who ends up writing a disparaging satire about Orlando, prompting the young man to turn back to society instead, lavishly refurbishing his home and hosting parties. To flee the unwanted advances of the Archduchess Harriet, he takes up an ambassadorial post in Constantinople where, suddenly, after a lengthy period of sleep, he finds himself transformed into a thirty-year-old woman. She spends some time travelling with Gypsies, before returning to England, where she discovers the advantages and disadvantages of being a woman. She meets the Archduchess again, who is revealed to be a man, the Archduke Harriet, but she rejects his marriage proposal. Time passes by quickly without Orlando ageing, and she lives through the eighteenth century, frequenting Pope, Addison and Dryden, and then the nineteenth, becoming disillusioned with the restrictions of the Victorian age. She marries the seafaring Marmaduke Bonthrop Shelmerdine, who then sets off on his travels. The novel ends in 1928, with Orlando finally publishing *The Oak Tree* and about to welcome back her husband.

Dismissed by some critics as nonsense or a frivolous *jeu d'esprit*, *Orlando* has now established itself as a ground-breaking and genre-defying piece of women's writing and investigation into the notion of gender. It was also a huge commercial success at the time, selling 10,000 copies in only a few months. Despite its fantastical story, however, the novel is relatively conventional from a formal point of view.

On 8th October 1931, Virginia Woolf published arguably her most experimental novel, *The Waves*; in fact, she did not even regard the book as a novel, describing it at the early stages of its composition as an "abstract mystical eyeless book: a playpoem". Initially entitled *The Moths*, the work, which ambitiously attempts to merge six individual consciousnesses into one, proved formidably difficult for her to realize. *The Waves*

Using intertwining interior monologues, the novel charts the progress from childhood to adulthood of six friends of contrasting dispositions, who are referred to only by their first names – Bernard, Louis, Neville, Jinny, Susan and Rhoda. It is structured in nine parts, each with a preamble poetically describing a seaside scene at a time of day symbolically relevant to the stage in the characters' lives portrayed in the corresponding part: the first part, dealing with childhood, begins with the depiction of an early morning, and so on. A central figure in all their lives is the charismatic Percival, a fellow pupil at the boys' boarding school: the six are reunited when they attend a dinner party in his honour just before he leaves to take up a colonial post in India – a rare moment of communion and unity between them – and they are all devastated when they learn that he has been killed there shortly afterwards. When they reach midlife they all separately have to deal with the reality of ageing, their own sense of failure and thoughts of death. Despite some friction between them, they experience another moment of togetherness at a second dinner, although this time it is laced with sadness and nostalgia. The final section of the novel is told entirely from Bernard's perspective, as he summarizes his life and that of the other characters to an acquaintance of his, disclosing what has happened to everyone – including Rhoda, who has committed suicide – and vows to keep on struggling against death.

Although the author herself was not satisfied with *The Waves*, and it has not quite reached the prominent position occupied in the Virginia Woolf canon by *Mrs Dalloway* and *To the Lighthouse*, it is seen by her admirers as the epitome of her formal experimentation and exploration of consciousness, as well as attaining new heights of lyricism. In any case, it was a commercial success at the time of its publication.

The Years   The last novel to be published during the author's lifetime was *The Years*, which came out with Hogarth Press in 1937. Its genesis was the considerably vaster project of incorporating political essays into a fictional narrative, begun in 1932 and which was to be called *The Pargiters*. However, Virginia then jettisoned the essay sections (which would find themselves in part used in her treatise *Three Guineas*) and reworked the book in a purely fictional form.

The novel spans half a century in the history of the Pargiter family, beginning in 1880 and ending in 1936, each chapter focusing on a specific year within that period. The first chapter, set in 1880 and the only one not to be limited to a single day, introduces the reader to the characters: the retired Colonel Pargiter, who is with his mistress; his wife, bedridden and on the verge of death; and their several children. The central event is the death and funeral of Mrs Pargiter and the various reactions within the family. In the snapshots of the Pargiters' lives provided by the following chapters, the reader finds out about the evolution of each character as the years go by. Amid these episodes concerning the family are glimpses of historical events, such as the death of Edward VII and the First World War. At the end of the book, the surviving Pargiters assemble for a family reunion.

After the vague, evocative lyricism of *The Waves*, Virginia Woolf here turned to fiction more explicitly anchored in a historical setting, and *The Years* is now considered an important examination of the nature and evolution of the female experience in the context of the growth of capitalism, war and modernity. Interestingly, it was the most popular of Woolf's novels in its day, perhaps because it largely dispensed with formal experimentation.

At the time of her suicide in April 1941 Woolf was working *Between the Acts* on another novel, *Between the Acts*; it was published without her final touches by Hogarth Press shortly after her death.

The story takes place in rural northern England in June 1939, on the day of an annual historical pageant that is to be performed on the grounds of the estate of Bartholomew Oliver. His daughter-in-law Isa, the romantic main character of the novel with a penchant for writing verse, has fallen out of love with her husband Giles and has her eye on Haines, a married local gentleman, something that arouses the surly Giles's ire. Another resident in Oliver's house is his eccentric sister Mrs Swithin, who spends the day in hectic preparations for the pageant, and the household is completed by two unexpected guests, the flirtatious Mrs Manresa and her apparently homosexual artist friend William Dodge. In the evening the pageant begins with a prologue and unfolds in four stages: "Great Elizabeth", an imitation of a romantic Shakespearean scene; the "Age of Reason", a pastiche of Restoration comedy; the "Victorian Age", which features a cockney policeman directing traffic at Hyde Park Corner before ordering a group of typically Victorian picnickers to disperse; and finally "Ourselves", a scene representing the present day and mainly consisting of a group of villagers turning mirrors on the audience.

While the short, eccentric novel *Between the Acts* has long been seen by some critics as failed and pointless, it is dense with allusion and wordplay, and self-conscious in its inclusion of a story within a story. This has opened many avenues of interpretation, especially when viewed in the context of its composition: the Second World War and its attendant anxieties.

Short Fiction   Throughout her career, Virginia Woolf also wrote short stories, which were often a testing ground for her innovative ideas for fiction, and were published in journals and magazines. In her lifetime she released one collection of short fiction, *Monday or Tuesday*, which was her first work for Hogarth Press and, appearing as it did in 1921, came at a crucial point in her artistic development: after the conventional *Night and Day* and before the experimental *Jacob's Room*. The eight pieces contained inside all explore the non-narrative side of fiction, all of them experimental yet highly structured. The title story 'Monday or Tuesday' uses the motif of a heron's descent to juxtapose various images and investigate the relationship between perceptions and truth. 'Kew Gardens' interweaves detailed descriptions of features of a botanical garden such as a snail's progress and flower beds with the conversations of a small group of characters; 'A Haunted House' contrasts the perceptions of a couple with those of the ghosts that also inhabit their house; 'A Society' is a satirical description of an upper-class party which gives rise to various vignettes; 'An Unwritten Novel' follows the musings of the narrator as she engages a fellow commuter in conversation on a train and speculates on her life; 'The String Quartet' describes in detail a recital and the surrounding circumstances; 'Blue and Green' is an exploration of colour and its objective and subjective associations; and 'The Mark on the Wall' uses the eponymous mark as a Proustian starting point for the narrator's reminiscences.

In 1944, Leonard Woolf published *A Haunted House and Other Stories*, an expanded collection, which included the stories mentioned above as well twelve additional ones, such as 'The New Dress' and 'The Duchess and the Jeweller', half of which had not previously appeared in print. The first collection of Virginia Woolf's complete shorter fiction, which also features her very first piece 'Phyllis and Rosamond' and the early incarnation of *Mrs Dalloway*, 'Mrs Dalloway in Bond Street', was published in 1985, running to over forty stories.

Virginia Woolf's first landmark essay on writing was 'Modern *Non-Fiction*
Fiction' (1919), in which she expounds her theory, crucial to
Modernism, that fiction should mimic life and concern itself
with the ordinary as well as the extraordinary and free itself
from the restraints of conventions such as plot:

> Examine for a moment an ordinary mind on an ordinary day.
> The mind receives a myriad impressions – trivial, fantastic,
> evanescent, or engraved with the sharpness of steel. From
> all sides they come, an incessant shower of innumerable
> atoms; and as they fall, as they shape themselves into the life
> of Monday or Tuesday, the accent falls differently from of
> old; the moment of importance came not here but there; so
> that, if a writer were a free man and not a slave, if he could
> write what he chose, not what he must, if he could base his
> work upon his own feeling and not upon convention, there
> would be no plot, no comedy, no tragedy, no love interest or
> catastrophe in the accepted style, and perhaps not a single
> button sewn on as the Bond Street tailors would have it. Life
> is not a series of gig lamps symmetrically arranged; life is
> a luminous halo, a semi-transparent envelope surrounding
> us from the beginning of consciousness to the end.

The notion that the description of consciousness is an end in
itself and not just a means to convey a traditional story would
infuse most of Woolf's fiction, even though *Night and Day*,
the novel that she published that same year, does not live up
to this radical new conception of writing. She would produce
more essays detailing her theories for a new approach to prose
fiction, such as 'Mr Bennett and Mr Brown' (1923), based on a
seminal talk entitled 'Character in Fiction', and 'Poetry, Fiction
and the Future' (1927).

Woolf pursued the subject of writing in the collection *The
Common Reader* (1925), a series of critical essays on literature
from Chaucer to Conrad (and including 'Modern Fiction').
Inspired by a quotation from Dr Johnson's *Life of Gray*, the
premise and uniting principle of these individual pieces is the
focus on the perspective of the average reader rather than that of
the professional critic or scholar. This position chimes with the
author's view of her herself as an outsider figure who challenged
the received historical narrative imposed by authoritarian male

scholarship, and the essays in general refrain from providing overarching critical frameworks, choosing to emphasize the personal, creative and pleasurable aspects of reading. This well-received collection was followed by another instalment in 1932, *The Common Reader: Second Series*, with essays organized and selected according to the same principles.

The other focus of Virginia Woolf's essay-writing was politics and the female condition (although a clear distinction between her literary and political writings would be an artificial one, as the two concerns tend to overlap). As seen above, the essay that most firmly established Woolf on the political map is *A Room of One's Own*, published on 24th October 1929 and consisted of a reworking of material from a series of lectures she had given in Cambridge the year before. The book attempts to explain how women writers have been historically marginalized by the patriarchy, by being denied the freedom, finances and education accorded to men. The author uses the fictional example of Judith Shakespeare, a theoretical sister of the great playwright, demonstrating the many ways in which her equal talent would have been prevented from expressing itself fully. In another section, the essay outlines a history of women's writing, examining the roles of authors such as Aphra Behn, Jane Austen, the Brontës and George Eliot. While being accepted as a fundamental cornerstone of the feminist canon, *A Room of One's Own* has since been criticized for the narrow category of women it delineates: educated female writers from affluent backgrounds.

The other political work worth mentioning in this brief outline of Woolf's non-fiction output is *Three Guineas*, published in June 1938 and recasting material originally destined for the *The Pargiters*. Written as a series of responses to letters, the treatise not only develops themes from *A Room of One's Own*, such as women's access to education and the professional world, but also goes beyond the previous work's scope by addressing one of the main anxieties of the time: war, which is depicted as another of the of the patriarchy's perversions and excesses. By tying feminism in with pacifism and anti-imperialism, *Three Guineas* would come to be regarded as another seminal political text.

Apart from literature and politics, another concern of Woolf's non-fiction (intrinsically related to the other two) is history and, more specifically, the genre of biography – an interest the young Virginia no doubt inherited from her father, Leslie Stephen. Apart from the countless biographical essays and sketches she wrote and her fictionalized biography of Vita Sackville-West, *Orlando*, not to mention the considerable autobiographical corpus constituted by her diaries, reminiscences and letters, Virginia Woolf produced two volume-length lives. The first, *Flush: A Biography*, published in 1933, is an account of the life of Elizabeth Barrett Browning's cocker spaniel, which, like *Orlando*, contains many elements of fiction. From the standpoint of the dog, the book addresses issues such as city life, creativity and the role of the female writer. Although not generally accepted among the novels in the Woolf canon, *Flush*'s status as a biography is also problematic, and the work has never met with popular success. The second, *Roger Fry: A Biography*, published in 1940, portrays her late friend and artist Roger Fry and is ostensibly a factual work, although it has been pointed out that Woolf's approach, while personal and insightful, does not fully adhere to conventional biographical rigour. This has often been seen has one of its charms, as the book eloquently and movingly describes the Bloomsbury Group and praises the virtues of friendship.

Select Bibliography

Virginia Woolf made several changes to *Jacob's Room* between the manuscript version and the final published form, including a number of cuts. *Virginia Woolf's Jacob's Room: The Holograph Draft*, ed. Edward L. Bishop (New York, NY; Oxford: Pace University Press, 1998), based on the manuscript in the Henry W. and Albert A. Berg Collection of English and American Literature at the New York Public Library, provides details of all the variants.

Biographies:
Bell, Quentin, *Virginia Woolf*, 2 vols. (London: Hogarth Press, 1972)
Gordon, Lyndall, *Virginia Woolf: A Writer's Life* (Oxford: Oxford University Press, 1984)
King, James, *Virginia Woolf* (London: Hamish Hamilton, 1994)

Lee, Hermione, *Virginia Woolf* (London: Chatto & Windus, 1996)

Rose, Phyllis, *Woman of Letters: A Life of Virginia Woolf* (Oxford: Oxford University Press, 1978)

Additional Recommended Background Material:
Majumdar, Robin and McLaurin, Allen, eds., *Virginia Woolf: The Critical Heritage* (London: Routledge, 1975)

Roe, Sue and Sellers, Susan, eds., *The Cambridge Companion to Virginia Woolf* (Cambridge: Cambridge University Press, 2000)

On the Web:
www.virginiawoolfsociety.co.uk
www.etudes-woolfiennes.org
www.utoronto.ca/IVWS

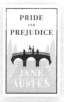

For our complete list and latest offers

visit

almabooks.com/evergreens

ALMA CLASSICS

ALMA CLASSICS aims to publish mainstream and lesser-known European classics in an innovative and striking way, while employing the highest editorial and production standards. By way of a unique approach the range offers much more, both visually and textually, than readers have come to expect from contemporary classics publishing.

LATEST TITLES PUBLISHED BY ALMA CLASSICS

www.almaclassics.com